The Pav

The Pawnbroker

A Horror Story

Stuart G. Yates

Also by Stuart G. Yates

- Unflinching

- In The Blood

- To Die in Glory

- Varangian

- Varangian 2 (King of the Norse)

- Burnt Offerings

- Whipped Up

- Splintered Ice

- The Sandman Cometh

- Roadkill

- Tears in the Fabric of Time

- Sallowed Blood

- Lament for Darley Dene

- The Tide of Terror

- Ogre's Lament - The Story of Don Luis

For my lovely daughter, Emily.
I'm so proud of you, the way you never give up
and always strive for the very best.
This one is for you, because you love a good horror,
from your dear old dad.

Contents

The Beginning

In the late 1860s, the narrow, twisting streets of the city were covered in thick grime which, like a leech, sucked everything good and wholesome from the very bricks and mortar of the surrounding buildings. A labyrinth of decay and unwashed humanity gave the warrens a particular stench, a cancer of filth, spreading remorselessly amongst the swarming populace. Here, people shared their lives with pestilence, rats and corruption. Having no chance for any other kind of existence, they accepted their plight without complaint and survived.

Life was cheap, as easily taken away as created, danger and death interlacing every breathing moment. That most wonderful of nature's gifts – the bringing of new life into the world – proved the most dangerous of times, for both mother and infant. Understanding of sickness, disease and infection remained rudimentary, doctors being as ignorant as they were a thousand years before. An accident could sever a limb, crush a bone or render a worker blind, thus ending any hope of placing food on the table. Necessity forced children, often as young as five or six, to work and keep everything in balance. Families were large, sharing crumbling dwellings with others, sometimes as many as twelve to a single room, crammed into airless, dank cellars. Parents hardly dared speak lest the youngest woke and set up endless wailing as the constant pain of hunger gnawed at the lining of their shrivelled bellies, sending mothers and fathers frantic with the noise. An unending nightmare, a constant struggle to make ends meet and get through just one more day.

Amongst this squalor, the pawnbroker roamed in his ephemeral undertaking. Flitting into people's homes and preying on their desperate need, he spied out valuable trinkets or family heirlooms, offering them a pittance for items worth a hundred times more. At least, as he often told them, he offered some relief to their pitiful existence.

"It's pearls," said the toothless crone, standing amidst the chaos of filthy, squabbling children, that morning in chilly autumn. The pawnbroker wrung his hands, seeming to fill the tiny room. Swathed in black, shoulders hunched, patient, he waited like some great predatory bird, his offer made. In the corner, a younger woman, perhaps the mother of the feral brood, rocked herself backwards and forwards, mumbling meaningless sounds. Both he and the crone ignored her.

Mouth widening slightly into what might be mistaken for a smile, the Pawnbroker's voice sounded as cold and as chill as a January morning. "You are mistaken, old woman. They are mere stones, polished to resemble pearls."

They held one another's stares. From out of the gloom, a man appeared, broad across the chest, huge arms dangling like an ape's, his eyes black-rimmed, breath stinking of drink. He shuffled forward, seizing the jewellery from the crone's grasp. "If she says it's pearls," he droned, words slipping from between wet, slack lips, "then it's pearls."

"I'll give you two shillings," said the pawnbroker, "and that is more than they are worth, even if they were real."

Such confrontations were bread and butter to the pawnbroker and he knew, in the end, his would be the triumph. He pulled in a long breath and dipped inside his pocket. The money jangled in his palm and the light in the big man's eyes raged. Licking his lips, voice thick, breath coming in short pants, he said, "Make it half-a-crown and they're yours."

A long, stretched-out moment followed, as the pawnbroker ruminated on the offer. Calculating the value of the pearls to be in excess of five pounds, he screwed up his mouth in a show of anguish. "Very well," he said at last and pushed the coin into the man's grimy fist whilst at the same moment relieving the crone of her treasure.

Outside in the stinking passageway, he allowed himself a chuckle of self-congratulation and ran the genuine pearls through his fingers. He must wait the mandatory fortnight, to give these desperate people the opportunity to return to his shop with the repayment, but he knew this was not likely; the half-crown would disappear down the big man's throat in a pint or two of gin. It was always the same. So, he'd hold onto them for a short time, before selling them on for a handsome profit. He had customers in Belgravia who would gladly give him well over the odds for such a string.

Hearing the footfall, he turned, alert and saw the oaf bearing down on him, those great, bearlike hands open, preparing to grasp and wrestle him to the ground, steal everything he carried. But the oaf, handicapped by drink, should have known better. The pawnbroker slipped inside those strong arms and sank his blade deep into the brute's side. The oaf gasped, incredulous, and the pawnbroker pressed his mouth close to his stricken attacker's ear.

"Hunger will no longer trouble you, my friend," he said and pushed the blade deeper still, the sharp blade slicing through internal organs. The big man groaned, a low, lamentable expulsion of fetid breath and the pawnbroker held him close, as one might an infant, and guided him to the ground, allowing the man's weight to free his body of the knife. Watching him crumple into a quivering heap, his life's blood leaking across the cobbles, the pawnbroker smiled and wiped his blade on the dying man's jacket before turning and disappearing into the maze of alleyways and side passages.

Gliding through the streets, he pondered on what had occurred. Usually, no one ever followed him. Such attacks were rare, most people grateful for the few coins he sprinkled into their eager palms. They would spend their money, perhaps on a few rotten potatoes, or more likely, if the husband caught wind of the transaction, on drink. Few attempted to win back their treasures. If ever they did, they failed, ending up like the big man – dead. None of this mattered to the pawnbroker. He remained unaffected by the deprivations he witnessed, the suffering, the violence. He traded in making money, accumulating his wealth, avarice his close companion. Nevertheless, he dreamed of discovering a truly valuable piece – a diamond-encrusted ring or necklace, anything that would transport him to the heady heights of comfort he so longed for and give him the means to escape this bleak, unrelenting existence.

In the close-knit community of his fraternity, his methods were causing concern. Pawnbrokers were not looked upon kindly by the desperate populace at any time, but he threatened to undermine even the very faintest sense of professionalism that some were attempting to create. There were rumblings, rumours and ramifications, and they summoned him to answer charges that he was bringing their profession into disrepute.

Unbeknown to his colleagues, the pawnbroker had already had a meeting. A meeting like no other. For too long, he had dwelt in the seedy, blackened world of sweaty, rundown offices. He had employed the talents of some local pickpockets, paying them well. They had crossed him, tried to swindle him, selling their ill-gotten wares for themselves and he'd reacted swiftly. A retribution both harsh and deadly. One damp and dismal morning, the bodies of two young boys, aged between eleven and thirteen, were washed up on the seashore at Egremont. Just nameless boys, lost to their parents many years before; both had had their throats cut. No one knew them and no one cared. The authorities undertook some sporadic investigations but, with little to go on, interest soon waned. They placed several posters around town – a meaningless gesture, for the majority of people who populated the neighbourhood could not read, and those that could bore them no mind. No one came forward and soon the bodies, wrapped up in coarse, jute sacks, were buried in a communal grave, forgotten.

A few weeks later, the pawnbroker employed another youth, a young lad by the name of Randolph, and at first things did not fare much better as he proved a useless pickpocket, almost getting himself caught more than once. Luckily for him, Randolph had seen something that might perhaps save him from the pawnbroker's wrath. Amidst the confusion of noise and crush of people that was Liverpool Pier Head, Randolph had spotted an interesting altercation between two men. One of them was as brown as a nut, but an Englishman nevertheless. Burly and tough-looking, he had berated a porter who had accidentally pulled one of the man's pieces of luggage onto the ground so awkwardly the sides had split. What Randolph saw nearly caused his eyes to pop out of their sockets. Jewels, a whole string of them, spilled out from the gash. The man was quick to stuff them back inside, whilst the porter hurriedly found some binding to lash around the leather case, but Randolph saw it all.

After the incident, and with the porter looking suitably shame-faced, Randolph followed the man, as expertly as he could, all the way onto the ferry that took him across the River Mersey to Birkenhead. From there, the man ordered a hansom cab and employed more porters to bundle the great case inside. Randolph, smart lad that he was, was close enough to hear the address.

The pawnbroker grinned when he heard the tale.

"This could be the one, my lad," he hissed, pouring himself a glassful of port wine by way of celebration. He didn't offer any to Randolph, but instead pressed a florin into the boy's hand. "There, you've done well. Now, I'm going to think up a little plan and then… then, I might be needing you again. Until then, you run along and leave me to my wine."

* * *

Randolph knew the pawnbroker's reputation all too well and he had no desire to cross him. If he could make as much as a florin every time the old man sent him out on a job, then that was enough for him. The thought of such earnings proved a wondrous one to Randolph, as he slipped out of the pawnbroker's lodgings and made his way along the streets towards the dockland area of Birkenhead. Bending his head to avert his eyes from any curious looks from passers-by, he did not know of Rooster's close proximity until he collided with the large midriff of the man. Randolph jumped, but was too slow to make good any escape attempt. Rooster had him by the throat in a blink, pinning him against the wall.

"Now then, little magpie," wheezed Rooster, his grizzled face close to the boy's, "tell me what you've been doing for our friend the moneylender. I followed you and I want to know what you and him are up to – be quick now, or I'll break your neck."

Those great, thick fingers squeezed and Randolph squawked, telling Rooster everything. And Rooster listened, and he, too, plotted.

* * *

That very evening, the pawnbroker stooped on bended knee before a large, gold incense burner of intricate design and, cupping the smoke with his hands, drew the intoxicating fumes closer to his face. The strange incantation was the one he always followed, taken from an ancient book passed to him many years before by a man from the Eastern part of Europe. It was a curious book, offered by a curious man.

Having come to the country some years before, the man, known only as Mancezk, found employment as the servant of a wandering magician, and assisted him in his travelling show. As they moved along the coast, from Blackpool down to Rhyl, people came and stood amazed at the flamboyant and mesmerising tricks the magician performed. But then, at one of the many bazaars on New Brighton pier, the magician mysteriously took ill and died. Some suspected poison, others the punishment of ancient, mystical gods. Whatever the truth, his servant gained the magician's possessions. Selling or discarding almost everything, Mancezk kept the book. He could not fully explain why, to himself or to anyone who might have asked. There was something magnetic about it and often he would wake in the middle of the night and reach out to stroke its green leather cover. Sighing as its creamy smoothness sent him in a state of bliss, he would sleep soundly until the morning.

Hard times struck and he sought out the pawnbroker and exchanged the book as surety against a small loan. Almost as soon as he held the book in his hands, the pawnbroker knew it was something special. Leafing through its pure velum pages, he felt a strange, preternatural stirring spread outwards from the pit of his stomach, to overwhelm every fibre of his being. That he could read it was a miracle, for the text was in some ancient tongue, long since lost, but a silent and powerful force guided him. A force which sought contact with an evil human entity. As for Mancezk, a Parish Beadle, on his way to check the veracity of a woman's claim of destitution to the Board of Guardians, found his body at the foot of an embankment, his throat cut deep, almost severing the head from the neck.

Now, having consumed almost the entire bottle of port, the pawnbroker sat, candles lit, a pentagram drawn upon the floor and recited the words. The incantations grew in intensity until, his voice rising in both volume and pitch, they became one continuous invocation of something dreadful. Inexorably, the atmosphere changed, an overwhelming chill spreading outwards from the centre of the room, and within it a blood-red glow containing a face – at one moment full, the next a flickering shade. Not the face of a human being, but the face of a creature beyond the realms of this world.

In the last few flickering moments before the candles burned out, the creature loomed forward. Hugely muscled, its head a swirling mass of protrusions, sharp, jagged, vicious-looking, limbs sinewy, imbued with preternatural strength, great hands clenching and unclenching. More massive than the solid granite of ancient mausoleums, this creature was related to death. It wallowed and celebrated in it, reeking of decay and corruption.

With eyes wide with wonder, the pawnbroker sat agog without recoiling, relishing the creature's presence. And its voice, rumbling, edged with wicked intentions, told the pawnbroker what he needed to do. As he listened, his soul grew hard. Even before this, the pawnbroker's soul was already lost, but now the creature claimed it for its own. In return, he imbued the pawnbroker with something more powerful and so much more seductive – pure evil.

"I'll do as I deem fit," he told those others of his profession who had summoned him to their enclave.

"Then you shall cease to part of our brotherhood," spat the chair of the meeting, a grizzled old man named Mathias, whose fortune was made through the desperation of the poor.

"You dare to think such a threat will divert me from my ambitions?" The pawnbroker levelled his gaze on each of the men assembled around the large table, the flickering oil lamps set in each corner casting their faces in deep shadow, distorting their features, making them seem more ghouls than human beings. He cackled, "I pity you."

"Pity *us*?" said Mathias, rising from his chair, knuckles pressing hard on the table top. "Damn your arrogance! You go too far in your dealings with the poor. You fill them with fear and then swindle them out of what miserable possessions they put in your way."

"You do much the same, so do not dare to preach to me, Nathanial Mathias."

"I keep my accounts transparent," returned Mathias, ignoring his colleague's barbed accusations, "as we all do in this room. But not you. No one knows where your dealings end up, or at what price."

"And there have been accusations," said another voice, floating out of the gloom. "Accusations of violence, or threats."

"Prove it."

"We don't have to prove it," said Mathias, "it is what we all know. Therefore desist, or you shall be barred from our profession, your license to trade revoked, and the authorities made aware."

The pawnbroker sat and considered the man's words.

He did not comment.

He merely slipped out of the room, leaving all of them to consider what might happen next.

Chapter One

The Old House

The present...

The two boys cycled up to the brow of the hill and stopped. They had been riding their bikes for a long time and both were almost out of breath. Perhaps, if they had turned their bikes around at that point, their lives would have been very different. Perhaps. But a dark and malevolent force was already at work, insidious and evil, utterly irrepressible and irresistible, making any independent decision unlikely, if not impossible.

Ignorant of any of this, for the time being at least, Jamie, the bigger of the two, looked at his friend. "I think we're lost," he said, his voice cracking with concern. "We'll never find our way home."

Tim, his friend, gave Jamie a look, eyes creased up, mouth pulled tight in a mocking smile. "What's the matter? Scared?"

"No," said Jamie, defensively, not able to return Tim's unwavering stare. "I'm not scared."

"Sure?"

"We've been riding for ages and I think we're lost." He did his level best not to reveal to Tim the worries flitting around inside him; worries which had been building for the last hour or so as he became aware of various features he felt sure they had ridden past more than once. "The woods… following the trail… it didn't seem right. Couldn't you feel it?"

Everything had started out fine. They had followed the main road that ran the length of the old wood, then Tim had spotted a gate that was almost hidden amongst the thickly overgrown gorse flanking it on either side. "Let's explore!" he had cried and, without waiting, he had rushed headlong through the entrance and along the path.

Jamie sighed. This was so typical of Tim, he thought; always impulsive, never stopping to think or consider the rights and wrongs of a situation. Jamie was so much more cautious. Well, that's how *he* saw it. A lot of his schoolmates would replace 'cautious' with 'boring'. He didn't want to appear like this to anyone, especially not Tim, so Jamie reluctantly followed, eying the old gate, half-hanging from its rusted hinges. Why had Tim brought him to this spot? And why had he just plunged on, regardless of any danger that might be lurking ahead? Jamie accepted he wasn't as adventurous as Tim, even though he was much older and bigger. Somehow, he just never seemed able to climb as well as Tim, or swim as well, or, more importantly, fight as well. Tim could do anything. Or at least that's how it all seemed to Jamie as he pushed forward, dismissing his fears.

Jamie knew he was lucky to have a friend like Tim. When most of the other boys at school called him names or simply ignored him, Tim remained his faithful companion. So Jamie tagged along, doing everything that Tim wanted to do. Even coming on this bike ride, to goodness only knew where.

After no more than fifty paces, the path narrowed, hyphenated by fallen branches and clumps of tangled bracken, forcing the boys to dismount. With his eyes glued on every step he took, Jamie felt the presence of the trees on either side, looming dark and dangerous, like a living thing, simmering hot within the press of undergrowth and soaring tree-trunks. Sweat lathered Jamie's face, his shirt clung to his back and his wet hands slipped from the handle-bars. Looking up briefly, he saw Tim's back as his friend strode resolutely on, and wished he could possess the same courage.

"I'm not sure about this," he said at last. "We said we'd be home by four." Looking at his watch, he raised his voice. "It's now nearly half-past." The idea of Mum being angry or, worse still, worried, was more of a concern for Jamie than the threat of Tim's displeasure.

Tim's voice, when he stopped and glared at him, seemed to echo Jamie's thoughts. "Half an hour late? Is that all you're worried about?"

"But it won't be half an hour by the time we get back, will it? It'll be more like an hour and a half."

Tim let out a long sigh, a scowl developing on his hard face. "If you're so bothered about what your mum will say, why don't you go home right now?"

Jamie's feeble resistance disappeared and he looked away, miserably admitting defeat.

"Besides," added Tim, "there's something ahead through here. Notice the way the trees thin out as if it's the beginning of a lawn or something? Let's go and have a quick look."

So they pushed on, emerging from the wood to stand in what might once have been a large, ornamental garden. The deliberate planting of big bushes here and there seemed to confirm this suspicion, but everything appeared tired and bedraggled, with weeds sprouting everywhere. Whoever had laid out the shrubs had long ceased tending them.

"If this is a garden," said Jamie, stepping up next to his companion, "that means it's private property and we're trespassing."

The garden's state of abandonment gave the surroundings a sinister air which, coupled with the almost complete and total silence of the woods, made Jamie feel uncomfortable, out of control, like a little, lost child. But before Jamie could offer an objection, Tim pressed on, ignoring him, stepping out from the darkness of the trees to take in more of the surroundings.

Jamie came up behind him and only just managed to stop before he crashed into Tim's back. Both boys stared at the house standing silent and enormous before them.

Tim whistled through his teeth.

"Whoa!" exclaimed Jamie.

The house loomed large and rambling, its great black and white walls towering upwards. It was built in a Tudor style, with large, panoramic windows that allowed those within to gaze upon the sprawling gardens. At some point in its history, this must have been a magnificent dwelling, throbbing with the comings and goings of important guests, a small army of servants dashing through its many rooms and corridors, the entire place alive with noise and expectation. Jamie wasn't sure how old it might be, but it certainly seemed in need of extensive repair; many of its windows appeared cracked, some of the timbers rotten. A lonely house, Jamie thought, not much sign of life, its grandeur nothing but a distant memory. It reminded him of something from a corny horror film and he didn't like it. He shuddered.

"Let's go and explore!" shouted Tim and, without waiting, he rushed forward, leaving his bike behind, racing across the unkempt lawn towards the main entrance.

Jamie raised his voice, calling, "Just a minute, Tim," but it was no use; Tim's mind was made up. Jamie shrugged, admitting defeat once again. He sighed and, pushing his bicycle, followed his friend.

A small hill ran up to the house. There was no sign of any fence or wall separating the grounds from the little wood out of which the two boys had emerged. Then Jamie realised – the boundary had been the gate they had gone through earlier. There had been no signs, at least none that he could remember, proclaiming that this was private property, so surely they wouldn't get into trouble simply because they were curious? But, as he approached the main doors, Jamie grew more uncertain, the awful thought they were trespassing pressing down upon him.

The closer he got, the bigger the house seemed, like some slumbering prehistoric beast. Its huge walls rose up to tower overhead, its great leaded windows peering down, all-seeing eyes watching their every move. Nevertheless, there were no apparent signs of life and when Tim pressed his face up against a window to look inside, Jamie followed.

There was nothing, just empty rooms. No furniture, no sign of habitation. Bare white walls, a sprinkling of broken plaster across the stripped wooden floors. "No one's lived in here for years," said Tim.

They moved on, keeping close to the building, Tim leading the way, all the way around to the far side of the house.

As they turned the corner, they stopped, and gasped. Before them lay a huge, open expanse of lawn stretching on into the distance. An impressive set of stone steps led down from a broad stone patio onto vast ornamental gardens, laid out in neat, geometric patterns, punctuated with several fountains in the midst of man-made lakes. Putting down his bike, Jamie edged forward as if in a trance and gazed out at the sprawling vista before him. The atmosphere of abandonment was acute, everything oddly empty, more like a still, lifeless photograph than actual reality. There was no sign of it having been looked after. In fact, it looked quite the opposite. No gardener had tended the lawns for many, many months, possibly years. Ornamental fountains stood silent, the lakes, which must have once been so crystal clear and sweet-smelling, were now stagnant and sterile. It was a depressing sight, made all the more so by the curious silence that hung heavy and threatening all around.

There was something about the fountain which beckoned Jamie to move forward; an irresistible force, urging him to investigate still further. He descended the wide steps, gaze fixed upon the sad, forlorn fountain decorated with three nymphs embracing one another, arms reaching skywards, faces alive with expectation.

"What are you doing, Jamie?"

Jamie shivered, dragging himself from his disturbing thoughts and turned to see Tim standing there, hands on hips. Jamie shrugged, the moment broken, and ran back to join his friend.

Together again, they both stood and stared, taking in the wide frontage of this magnificent edifice, in the centre of which loomed enormous double-doors, black with age, with an impossibly huge brass door knocker set in the middle. Waiting. But for what?

Massive, leaded windows flanked the huge entrance. The two boys exchanged a look. Tim licked his dry lips and then, seeming to reach some decision within himself, took a deep breath and curled his fingers around the metal handle.

"What are you going to do?" whispered Jamie frantically.

Tim smiled back at him, a mocking smile full of contempt. "Knock at the door, idiot."

Jamie looked about him. Nothing stirred, either from the garden or from the tree-line, yet that sense of somebody watching crept over him again and he shivered. The entire place was just too creepy for words.

He started as Tim rapped the heavy metal knocker against the door.

The sound boomed through the house.

They waited, hearts thumping.

There was no answer.

"Let's go," said Jamie quickly, his voice barely a whisper.

Tim grinned. "Don't be soft," he mocked, "I'll give it another go." And he did, a harder, louder knock this time.

Again they waited, listening intently to the gradually fading sound echoing throughout the huge interior.

Nothing.

Tim turned to his friend and shrugged his shoulders. "No one in."

Jamie closed his eyes, releasing a long sigh of relief. "Oh, that's good. Let's go home now. At least we won't get in any trouble from the owners."

Tim shook his head. "What are you on about now?"

"Well, it's obvious, isn't it? That gate we came through, it must have been the entrance to this place."

"Well, of course it was, you potato head."

"Yes, and no one stopped us because no one is in." Jamie struck a pose, hands on hips, chin jutting out, looking smug. "So, let's go home before they get back."

"Why? What could they do?"

"Er… get us arrested?"

Tim ignored the sarcasm in Jamie's voice. "I'm going to try the door, see if it's open."

As his fingers closed again around the huge, bulbous door handle, Jamie, gripped by an irresistible impulse, jumped forward and tore Tim's hand away.

"No," he said, his voice cracking with fear, "no, Tim. You mustn't."

"You're such a wimp," said Tim, sounding angry. He gave Jamie a sharp push in the chest, sending him staggering backwards. He landed awkwardly on the ground, too shocked to feel any pain, more embarrassed and surprised at his friend's unexpected show of force. The fact Tim could turn like that made him question other things, too. His friend appeared determined not only to explore, but to break in. But then, as Jamie climbed slowly to his feet, he noticed Tim had frozen in the act of turning the handle. All thoughts of the injustice he felt at Tim's assault dwindled away, replaced by a strange tingling at the base of his neck. There was something wrong. "What's the matter?" he whispered, hardly daring to speak.

Tim turned and looked at him, his eyes wide. "It's unlocked," he gasped and then, without a moment's hesitation, he pushed the huge door open and stepped inside.

Chapter Two

Message from the Past

As the two boys stood side by side in the massive hallway, the silence, eerie and unnatural, pressed against them, seemingly from the very walls themselves. The atmosphere grew cold, forcing them both to shiver, their breath steaming from trembling lips. They exchanged looks.

"There's something very wrong in here," whispered Jamie.

For the first time that day, Tim agreed, offering a feeble nod. "It feels so lonely."

The wide entrance hall ran towards a broad staircase, the steps of which were bare white wood. It curled upwards and around to the right, the balustrade, like the walls and everything else, appearing cracked along its surface, its ancient paint blistering and peeling. Beneath their feet, the tiles were thick with dust and the air reeked with the thick, clammy smell of damp. "No one's going to disturb us," said Tim, turning to his friend. "Nobody has been in this house for years."

This observation should have given Jamie some sense of comfort, but all he experienced was a sense of growing dread. He peered upwards to the ceiling and shivered. "It's like the house is telling us to 'get out'."

"Don't be daft. Houses aren't alive."

"This one is, I know it."

"You're letting your imagination run wild, Jamie." Tim forced a laugh, but to Jamie it sounded strained, almost as if his friend were putting it on, trying to present a brave face. "It's old and it's empty – and that's it."

"But the air, it's so heavy – like lead. It's full of … *something*. Danger. Can't you feel it?"

If Tim did, he didn't admit it. "I can't feel a thing," he said and pointed down the hallway. "Let's explore a little more." Without waiting for an answer, he pressed on.

Sighing, Jamie reluctantly followed his friend to the staircase which ascended into the gloom. To the left of the stairs stood a closed door and farther down on the right, two more, also closed, their harsh whiteness like an immovable barrier, giving out a bleak warning – *DO NOT ENTER.* Turning away, Jamie surveyed the immediate area. Everywhere, the dim outlines of shapes danced in darkened corners, features barely discernible in the half-light. Deep shadows lurked in every mysterious recess.

Unable to ignore the dread growing inside him, Jamie took breath and tapped Tim on the shoulder, saying quietly, "I think we should go."

With one foot on the first tread, Tim's face twisted into a scowl. "Are you nuts?" he whispered harshly. "This place is fantastic. It's like something out of an old history book. Hey, perhaps that's it – we've gone back in time hundreds of years."

"Don't be stupid, it's just an empty house." Jamie looked along the blank walls, noticing the faint outlines where once paintings had hung. "Abandoned." On impulse, he tried one of the light switches; nothing happened. "Anyway," he continued, "I don't think it's *that* old. It's like one of those houses we talked about in school when we did the Victorians. I'd say it's only about a hundred years old."

Tim screwed up his nose. "Ugh, I hated the Victorians. I thought the Vikings were better." He suddenly leapt around pretending he was hacking at an enemy with an imaginary battle-axe. "All those raids and battles – it was great, not like the rubbish we do now." He noticed Jamie watching him and shook his head sadly, then stopped his play-acting and grinned. "Come on, stop being such a bore – let's have a look around."

"No. We shouldn't, Tim. It doesn't feel right." As if to give weight to his words, he gave an involuntary shudder.

"You're just a wimp."

Good-humoured or not, Tim's words hurt. The moniker hung around his neck as if it were a label, emblazoned with huge, pulsating letters: *WIMP*. Everyone whispered it behind his back; those callous and brave enough said it to his face. Wincing, he turned from Tim's gaze. "Let's just go. We've been really lucky so far, but what if the owners come back? We could get into loads of trouble." His words sounded hollow knowing, as he did, that the place was deserted.

"Jamie, you said so yourself – there's no one around. Okay, so it's been looked after, but not for a long time – there's no electricity, no heating, nothing. It's not someone's home any more, is it?"

"So what is it then?"

"I think it's been left empty and somebody just comes in and tidies up every now and then. Look at the state of the gardens. If somebody lived here, they'd have all the flowers nicely looked after and the grass cut."

"Maybe the owners can't afford it," suggested Jamie quickly, desperate to find any reason why they shouldn't stay, despite the fact that Tim's words made perfect sense. "It must have cost a fortune to keep this place going. Imagine the running costs – as well as all the servants."

Tim looked around him, a frown creasing his brow. "Yeah, maybe you're right, but…" He tilted his head to the stairs and peered into the gloom. "Something must have happened, something pretty big, for the owners to leave a place like this. There's no furniture, no carpets… you can even see where the pictures have been." He rubbed his finger around the shadow of a former painting. "It all happened a while ago, I reckon."

"But what could have caused them to leave it like this? Business failure, scandal …?"

Tim shrugged and turned to look at his friend again, "What does it matter? I'm not all that bothered about the reasons, to be honest. This place is like a great big adventure playground, and who knows, we might even find some treasure."

"Treasure? They're not likely to have left anything of value behind, are they?"

"You never know." Tim brought his hand down sharply on Jamie's shoulder. "We're going to have some fun exploring this place, so come on."

Before Jamie could react, Tim, ignoring the stairs, disappeared through the door on his left, leaving Jamie alone and afraid. Hesitating, he watched, mesmerised, as the door gently closed as if of its own volition. Now that he was alone, the house seemed to grow larger around him, the ceiling yawning wide above him, the walls like huge arms reaching out to wrap themselves around him, squeezing the life from his body. Crying out Tim's name, he pushed open the door and rushed ahead, heedless of what waited for him beyond the threshold.

What waited was a room, much narrower and longer than he expected to find, sunlight streaming through three tall, unshuttered windows which ran along one side. The glass was grey with grime, blocking out the view outside. Squinting through the dusty air, he managed to make out the imprint of a great table that had once dominated the room, with several chairs standing around it, their impressions still clearly discernible on the bare floor. A dining room fit for a lord and lady.

Not willing to disturb the film of dust too much, he carefully crossed to the windows and made a small peephole in the dirt of the closest pane with his finger. Peering through this, he caught sight of the sweeping fields surrounding the house, rolling down as they did to the line of trees out of which the two boys had emerged moments before. He sucked in his breath, the blackness of the trees surprising him. What time was it? Surely, it couldn't already be evening?

He turned away from the window and, looking towards the far end, spotted a statue. He wondered why he hadn't noticed it as soon as he had entered the room, for it was large, carved from white marble. The figure of a woman, hair cropped short, it had one arm reaching forward, palm uppermost, in the act of offering something, the other broken off above the elbow.

Without thinking, previous caution ignored, Jamie strode directly towards it. At its base was a small plaque in the shape of a scroll, engraved with writing. Squatting down on his haunches, he tried to make out what the inscription said, but thick dust prevented a quick read. So, pulling the cuff of his sweat-shirt over his hand, he briskly rubbed away the film of dirt to reveal a sort of poem:

For the years we had together
and the memories we will always share,
my heart and soul are yours
forever.

Jamie was a good reader, the best in his class when he was in Primary, but the writing puzzled him. Why would anyone leave a thing of such obvious importance behind after stripping the rest of the house bare? Leaning closer, he read it again – simple words that said so much about a life shared, a life of devotion and love. Craning his neck, he considered the form of the woman looming over him. It was so large that it would be difficult to move, but even so, with the delicate use of a chisel in skilled hands, the inscription could have been removed. Unless, of course, something had happened to make the meaning behind the message worthless? Something that had forced the two... two what? Lovers? They had to be, given the words. Perhaps an argument had torn them apart, leaving them bitter, resentful, neither wanting such a memory to continue in their new life. Jamie couldn't tell, but he guessed the answer was probably very simple – the statue had proved too big or too heavy to take with them.

He reached forward and, tracing his finger around the edge, realised the plaque was part of the stone from which the stature had been carved. So any attempt to cut it free, even by an expert, would have meant the virtual destruction of the entire piece. Old people went into 'old people's homes' when they reached a certain age and independent living became impossible. No longer able to cope on their own, they would end up in a single room where space was limited. That was where Jamie's gran had ended up – first in sheltered accommodation, then later in a home. The memory caused a shudder to run through him as he remembered Gran's frightened face pleading with his mum not to leave her there, to let her go back to the home she knew.

Blowing out a loud sigh, he stood up. Studying the statue carefully, his eyes lingered on the broken arm. A clean break, the marble smooth. Maybe it was deliberate, a Venus de Milo attempt to create something special. But one arm remained and, without thinking, he brushed her palm with his fingers and marvelled at how warm it felt. As if it were alive...

He pulled himself up sharply, forcing himself from his reverie. Rubbing his chin, he turned his thoughts to Tim, remembering that his friend had come into this room first. But there was no sign of him. Then, in the far right corner, he spotted another door. Glancing to the floor, Jamie saw the tell-tale signs of footprints in the dust, so, without another thought, he strode towards the door, grasped the handle and pulled.

The door was locked.

For a moment, every muscle froze. If he could have found the strength, he would have cried out, but fear was draining his energy. So he waited, trying to muster up the courage to try again. It was a mistake, a misjudgement. It couldn't be locked. It *couldn't*....

Desperately, he rattled the handle, seized with sudden, uncontrollable panic. "Tim!" he shouted, no longer caring if anyone heard him. "Tim, are you in there?" Another bout of furious tugging brought no change – the door remained firmly closed. Biting down the tears, with both fists he set up a wild pounding, his voice trembling as he cried, "Tim, please, open the door!"

When no answer came from within, he pressed his face against the cold woodwork and allowed despair to overwhelm him. Tears tumbled down his cheeks, his body heaved with sobs and his throat, constricted with terror, groaned out a pathetic, whimpering, "Tim, *please...*" If this was his friend's idea of a joke, it was the cruellest possible prank.

Fishing out his mobile phone, he jabbed at the 'quick-dial' before seeing there was no signal. He groaned, waving the phone frantically in the air like it was a fan, like that would work. It didn't. The screen remained black. Defeated, he slipped it back into his pocket.

Seized with renewed vigour, or perhaps simply blind panic, he reared up, hammering once more against the door, continuing until his fists throbbed with pain, until the strength leaked out of him.

And again, no response.

Surrendering to the inevitability that neither Tim nor anybody else was going to open the door, he turned and, wiping his face with the back of his sweatshirt-covered hand, he searched the room, hoping against hope that there might be another exit, some other means of leaving the room – a window or cupboard, anything that might have offered Tim an escape route. But there was nothing. Crushed with the awfulness of the situation, he crumpled at the knees, sliding down the door to the floor, and covered his face with his hands.

There was no escaping the terrible truth pressing in all around him.

Jamie was quite, quite alone.

Chapter Three

Dreamtime

Jamie sat with his back to the door, his eyes red raw, stinging from prolonged crying. Without his friend beside him, he felt mortally afraid and more vulnerable and alone than ever before in his life. If only Tim had listened to him, they could both be at home by now, tucking into their tea, laughing together, looking forward to another bike ride the following day. But Tim *never* listened to him and the consequence of this was that everything that could go wrong had gone wrong. Now, Tim was lost and Jamie was all by himself in this wretched room. As a new bout of sobs welled up from the back of his throat, he couldn't imagine a worse situation to be in.

Slowly, the realisation of the utter uselessness of shedding tears brought a new, simmering anger to replace his fear. Anger at his own weakness more than anything else. He should have insisted that he and Tim went home and, if Tim's determination to go on continued, then he, Jamie the wimp, should have simply picked up his bike and pedalled home. He might have lost his only friend, but he wouldn't be experiencing the awfulness he now faced. With a sudden resolution, he wiped his eyes with the back of his sleeve and climbed to his feet.

"No use sitting here," he said to himself, his voice sounding tinny in that cold, sparse room, He padded over to the door leading led back into the main hallway. For a moment, he was seized by an irrational dread of finding this door locked as well. Biting down on his bottom lip, breath held, he eased the handle down and released a long sigh of relief as it swung open.

The hall appeared as before, except for the light. Already, evening was coming on, the stark, whiteness of the walls changing to a more subtle, softer grey. They appeared to undulate, moving in and out of focus, and, a little light-headed, he fell back against the wall, pressing thumb and finger into his eyes. When at last he looked again, the walls were solid, albeit a deeper shade of grey. Swallowing down his panic, Jamie calculated he had two choices before the darkness trapped him here – to leave his friend in the house, cycle back home and tell Mum, who would almost certainly call the police, or to find Tim himself.

Both ideas filled him with dread, but it didn't take him long to decide that leaving Tim all alone in this great, creepy edifice wasn't the right thing to do. Taking a deep breath, he shuffled towards the great stairway, and, reaching the bottom step, looked up.

They were steep and tall, curving slightly to the right near the top before they met the landing, which disappeared into the deepening gloom. He swallowed hard. He'd always been afraid of upstairs, ever since he could remember; dark, foreboding, full of the terrors of the night. His own house was a Victorian terrace, full of creaks and groans, but these stairs led to something infinitely scarier. The unknown.

Despite his dread, he knew he had little choice and, resigned to finding his friend, there was only one answer. He began to climb upwards.

The bare wooden boards creaked horribly with every step he made. Occasionally, he stopped and waited, hardly daring to breathe, feeling sure he would hear something. The closing of a door, the shuffling of feet. So he listened, tilting his head, mouth open, senses alert. Nothing came back to him, not even birdsong from outside. And yet, he could not shift the feeling that someone, or *something,* was watching him, observing his every move. More unnervingly, he felt that whoever it was laughed at him, mocking his weak and spineless nature. 'Go home,' the silent voice seemed to be calling, urging him to turn and run, 'Go home!' Dragging a trembling hand across his brow, he drew in a full breath, and continued upwards.

At last, he reached the top. Hoping against hope, he felt for the light switch to his left, but knew nothing would happen when he pressed it on. He was right and he paused for a moment, indecisive. To continue meant moving ever deeper into the darkness, a darkness which developed with every passing second. But he had no choice. Pressing himself against the wall, he took a breath and edged forward, ignoring the doors, deciding Tim would not have gone through any of them. He knew many old houses such as this one had connecting stairs that servants would have used. This was his hope – to find a second set which might lead him back to the dining room, and that damned locked door. Tim would have used this as his escape route and maybe, just maybe, his friend would be waiting there for him.

As he progressed along the landing, however, it dawned on him that no such second staircase existed, at least not here. Doors. Nothing but doors, but leading to where? The place was like a maze and he had no idea where any of the doors might lead. Soon, he wouldn't be able to see a thing. Already, his hand was little more than a smudge in front of his face. As the darkness became complete, he would be stranded here, with nowhere to go. So, with this thought displacing all others, he reached for the nearest door and pulled at the handle.

It was locked.

He couldn't help but snigger. So typical of his luck, so typical of everything that had gone wrong since stepping into this gaping mausoleum of a house.

Without pausing, he moved on down the hallway at a half run, trying each door in turn. They all remained firmly closed and when he reached the far end, where the landing turned, he pulled up short and gasped. As he squinted into the gloom, the horror of what he managed to see threatened to pitch him over into total panic.

A dead end.

Knowing he could not stop his search, he turned, determined to try them all again. He had to be missing something. Surely there was a way through? There had to be. He wanted to shout out, demand Tim return, but unbearable fear prevented him from doing so – the fear that his own voice might bring down a legion of demonic creatures upon him, clamouring for blood.

He stopped, squinting again into the gloom of the corridor and the dead end. What if it wasn't dead? It didn't make sense – a hallway leading to nowhere? His breathing, which by now was more like panting, rumbled through the narrow confines of the passageway. Fear mingled with despair. But he had to see, he had to know. There was nothing to lose and perhaps a lot to gain, so he strode on, certain his suspicions would prove right – and they did.

A door, towards the far end. So easily missed in the dark.

Allowing himself a smile of self-satisfaction, he pressed down on the handle… and it opened.

Relief swept through him at a rush, causing him to feel giddy, and he held onto the handle and waited, mastering his breathing, calming himself down. He eased the door open and scanned the interior, a window on the far side allowing sufficient light for him to make out the details.

Unlike the dining room, pieces of beautifully crafted furniture filled every space. And in the centre, dominating everything, was a large bed, festooned with a clutch of soft pillows, a thick padded quilt of sumptuous satin lying unruffled across it. Next to it stood a small bedside cabinet, a lamp with a red tasselled shade placed on top. If this was any other house, Jamie would have thrown himself down amongst the thick covers and fallen asleep straight away. But this was unlike any other house he had ever experienced. And this room, why was it so furnished, almost as if it was waiting for him, or some other random visitor, to discover it?

Uneasily, half expecting someone to loom out from a corner, he crossed to the window and pressed his nose against the glass. But although he was high up, the encroaching night made picking out any features impossible. By now, his mum would be going wild with worry, so he pulled out his mobile phone and went to punch out his mum's number and stared in disbelief. This time, not only was there no signal, but the battery appeared dead. In desperation, he waved the phone in front of the window, but with no success. Putting his palms under the sash, he strained with all his strength to force it open, but it would not budge. Layers of paint, built up over the years no doubt, sealed it tight.

With a sigh, he flopped down on the bed.

It felt good.

So comfortable.

Before Jamie knew what he was doing, all his anxieties and worries slipped away, forgotten. He lay back amongst the soft, warm, inviting covers and closed his eyes. A sudden heavy, irresistible drowsiness smothered him in its comforting embrace and before very long, he drifted off to sleep.

Interlude

Reeling down a grim, grimy passageway, Randolph stopped, sucking in his breath, and gingerly felt the raw flesh where Rooster's gnarled hand had squeezed him – squeezed him as tight as a lemon. With his eyes watering uncontrollably, he stumbled on, all sense of place and direction lost. A few people snarled at him as he barged into them before staggering down a high brick walled passageway, but he paid them little heed, anxious to get away as fast as he could. The memory of Rooster, his massive frame looming over him with those great, frying-pan hands, frightened him beyond measure. Within the time it took to take a breath, he gave up everything, every detail he could remember, and what he couldn't, he invented. And now he knew, as sure as night followed day, that if the pawnbroker discovered, or even guessed at, what he had done, that would be it. He'd be dead.

He couldn't make his mind up who was worse – Rooster or the pawnbroker. Both were sons of the Devil, of that he had no doubt. Capable of anything, even murder. He'd brought all of this upon himself, of course he had. He should have kept his greedy mouth shut. Instead, here he was, crushed by two of the most dangerous men in the city.

Chest heaving, more from fear than exhaustion, he slid down the chipped brick wall onto a doorstep and stared at his bare, filthy feet. Why had he run away from the workhouse all those months ago? Why hadn't he stayed and done the best he could? At least he was safe in there, he had food, a roof above his head. Now he had nothing, his only companion fear, and the promise of violence to come.

The door behind him creaked open and an old hag emerged and cursed at him, lashing out with a broom. Without a backward glance, he sprung to his feet and ran, his mind made up – he'd have to get away again, just as he had from the workhouse, only this time somewhere far away. So far, nobody would ever find him... farther than he'd ever gone before.

* * *

But eyes were watching Randolph. Virulent, all-seeing. They knew where to look, every move carefully scrutinised, nothing left to chance.

The hand came from nowhere, silent as the night, and took Randolph by the throat, crushing his larynx with a force not limited by this world, power far beyond anything Rooster had exerted, lifting him off the ground. Slammed hard against the wall, Randolph tried to pull the steel fingers away, but it was useless. His legs thrashed out desperately. He knew, as his limbs went limp and his body sagged, that his life was close to being snuffed out. A cry, nothing more than a gargle, died in his throat and then he stopped, eyes bulging, and saw and watched in stupefied horror as the pawnbroker brought his face close, cackling. "I'll not let you die yet, young Randolph," he said, "not until you tell me everything."

By now, the darkness was so intense that Randolph could barely make out the man's features, but he knew the voice and that was enough. He gagged and the vice-like grip relaxed, just a notch.

The voice took on a mocking, theatrical tone. "Did you tell him what you saw, Randolph? Did you tell him about the jewels?"

Though he struggled to formulate a lie, Randolph's eyes held the answer and the pawnbroker tutted in mock disappointment.

"Oh deary, deary me. Still, couldn't be helped, eh? No doubt he threatened you, did he?"

"Yes," gasped the boy, his voice little more than a rasp. "Yes, he did. Big, fat, ugly monster that he is. Said he'd break my neck, he did. He said he'd –"

The pawnbroker pressed a long, thin finger against the boy's lips. "Randolph. Fear is not something to be ashamed of. It does strange things. Makes you do what you wouldn't ordinarily do. Not in the wider meaning of things. If you understand me."

Randolph didn't and he shook his head grimly.

The pawnbroker released his grip and the boy fell back against the wall, clutching at his throat. "You told him about the... *jewels?*"

The boy nodded. "I – I didn't mean to... he made me. Like I said, he –"

"Sssh. Don't go into apoplexy, my lad. So, he knows about the jewels, the house, where it is located... everything."

"I'm sorry."

"Sorry?" The Pawnbroker cocked his head. "I gave you a florin for your hard work, Randolph. What did Rooster give you?"

"Nothing."

"Nothing? Doesn't seem fair, does it. Him getting all of that precious information for nothing. Seems like I'm out of pocket."

Quickly, Randolph fumbled inside his trousers and brought out the shiny coin. The pawnbroker took it, eying it keenly.

His white, skeletal hand disappeared into the folds of his great, thick overcoat and reappeared, the long, evil-looking blade catching something from the sky. Moonlight? Starlight? Randolph didn't care, all his attention fixed on its sharpness. He crumpled, whimpering, arms coming in up a pathetic attempt to ward off what he knew was about to happen.

Another short laugh creaked from the pawnbroker's mouth. Cold and callous. Without conscience. Like his voice. "Just desserts, eh? A story told, a story shared, a story... *lost*!"

They were to be the last words Randolph ever heard in this world.

* * *

In the miserable confines of his office, the pawnbroker sat beside his ledger some hours later, scrawling the day's receipts with a spidery hand. Throwing down his pencil, he closed the great book with a resounding slap and stretched out his arms to relieve the ache between his shoulders. The plan was hatched and soon the conjured-up forces would work with him to deliver the bounty.

He grinned.

Soon.

Chapter Four

Bert

Dreaming...

Albert Spiers, known to his friends as Bert (or Burrt, as Mr Rooster often pronounced it, stretching out the single vowel of his name) sat on the old wall, legs dangling, listening to the sound of the river, throwing tiny stones into one of the nearby puddles created by the recent downpour. The rain turned everything grey, including the wall upon which he sat. It was a crumbling wall, all that was left of a once popular and thriving gin-palace. Not so very long ago, Bert would linger outside, offering to help the drunks on their way whilst dipping their pockets with his expert hands. But then the fire burned the place to the ground, putting his lucrative sideline to rest. Still, the memories were good and he would often, as now, sit on the wall and reflect.

This particular grey and miserable day, he waited for Josh. Josh, who was late. Bert considered a Peeler might have nabbed his friend. If that were the case, then old Cock-bird, as he called Mr Rooster behind his back, would be none too happy. Mr Rooster expected money today, and if no money was forthcoming, then Bert would feel the weight of the big man's fist behind his ear. Unconsciously, he pulled at his earlobe and shivered at such an unsettling thought.

He cast his mind back to two or three years ago, when his drunken father put an empty gin bottle across mother's face. He remembered her scream as the glass smashed, lacerating her face, creating an instant, bloody latticework of disfiguration. One of the larger shards sliced through her jugular and he remembered watching her in stunned silence as she fell to the ground, her body writhing uncontrollably, the blood pumping through her fingers as she tried desperately to stem the tide. And Father, standing blubbering, staring at his dying wife, the broken glass slipping from his shaking hand. Nothing he could do now, the deed done. There were only regrets. And fear.

He had turned jaundiced eyes towards his eldest and screamed, sending a spray of spittle towards him, like a net, to catch and draw him in.

Bert ran.

He never stopped to think of his tiny brother, Patrick. Eighteen months old. How would he survive, how would Father cope, how would Mother…?

That very night, as he lay collapsed amongst the cotton bales in a dockside warehouse, a big man had appeared out of the darkness, his fat face full of smiles and reassurances.

Rooster.

Rooster took him in, gave him fresh clothes, food, a place to stay. All he needed to do in return was rob. From the rich. Like he was supposed to do today. Him and Josh. But Josh had decided, for whatever reason, not to show up. So here he was, worried sick, sitting on a crumbling old gin-palace wall. Now, there was an irony. Gin. Not only 'Mother's Ruin', but everyone's. He sighed and offered up a prayer to the one they called Jesus. He was meant to be important and could grant wishes, if you prayed hard enough. Bert did so now, praying for Josh to appear.

If he could read, Bert would have noticed that on the wall opposite were numerous bills, only recently posted. Many were the usual advertisement pamphlets, but one was a police notice. It didn't bear any picture, only an ominous warning:

Be aware that a kidnapper is known
to frequent this area. Any person having any
relevant information regarding the
disappearance of numerous BOYS should contact
their local constabulary. Ransoms are known to have
been made and suspicion of MURDER having been committed.
Reward for any information leading to an arrest.

Because no picture accompanied the words of warning, Bert paid it no heed.

He should have done.

* * *

Time moved on. Several people shuffled along the street, their faces buried deep inside large-collared overcoats. A little girl tried to sell matches to the passers-by but no one would buy. Across the way, sprawled over the steps of a shop, an old woman lay huddled amongst a pile of old and ragged blankets. She hadn't moved for ages. Bert thought that she might be dead. No one paid her any attention, and neither did he after a few moments. She wouldn't have any money so she was of no interest to him. Just another weary traveller come to the end of a not very eventful, but extremely hard life.

Bert sighed again, louder this time. This was not like Josh. Patience at an end, he swung himself off the old wall, repositioned his cap, rammed his hands deep into his threadbare pockets and, after one last look around, entered the warren of twisting, winding back streets that led him away from the seafront and the proposed place he and Josh were meant to visit together.

Finally, he emerged into the town centre, squeezing through the press of people moving along the wide pavements like one enormous animal. He knew this time was known as 'rush hour', the best part of the day for thieves and pickpockets to operate. Tired office and shop workers, making their way home to their damp and dreary terraces, their minds on warm fires and steaming bowls of potato stew. Bert took a quick glance towards either side of the street and darted out into the frenzied mass of horse-drawn vehicles as they squealed, groaned and clattered their way over the cobbles. Horses whinnied, drivers shouted and Bert saw his chance. With well-oiled skill, he dipped between some carriages and leapt up behind the furthest one, hitching a ride on the back of an old trolley bus as it trundled by. No one saw him. Even if they had, they probably wouldn't have said anything. Guttersnipes stole rides all the time.

At Hamilton Square, he managed to scoot off just as the driver did notice him, and then he was gone, running down a side street, disappearing into the smoky blackness of soot-encrusted brick.

He kept close to the river because this was the part of town he knew best. He ran all the way, his face looking down, avoiding the glances of the curious. Mr Rooster had taught him that and Mr Rooster had been to London and learned it all! Mr Rooster had told him stories of arrests and near-arrests, of being arraigned before courts of law, of being thrown into stinking, filthy prison cells. He taught Bert the value of not being caught and not being noticed. He taught him how to appear polite and deferential, never to answer back or appear surly. That was the one, sure-fire way to attract the wrong type of attention. So, he became nondescript, featureless, nothing more than a flicker in the corner of people's eyes. Right now, he needed all his guile, all his acting skills. He did his best to appear like any other normal boy, making his way steadily home. Pacing himself in an easy, loping gait, Bert jogged along until the noise of the big town subsided, the buildings became fewer, the urban surroundings giving way to a more rural aspect. Following the road, not quickening or slackening his pace, he reached the spot where they had put the barrow only two nights before, as a sort of sign in case they forgot the exact position of entrance.

Once, perhaps half a century ago, this entrance would have looked magnificent. Large, tall iron gates, intricately rendered in a lattice pattern, now largely concealed by a mass of overgrown bushes, perhaps deliberately allowed to spread across the metalwork to keep it secret. But the boys found it.

Stopping, Bert checked the barrow. It hadn't been moved. He peered into the depths of the woodland beyond the gate.

Still no Josh.

Bert cursed. He'd felt sure that Josh would be here, no doubt with some cock and bull story to explain why he hadn't turned up at the pier. But Bert was on his own and he had little choice in what he had to do. Mr Rooster expected nothing less than results and, however difficult the next few hours may prove to be, Bert would have to try his utmost to bring back what old Cock-bird wanted – money. He spat into his hands, took a firm grip on the handles of the barrow and began to heave it up towards the large iron gates.

Pulling apart tendrils of thick, matted ivy, he sought out the great bell hanging from the side pillar and, tugging the dangling cord from side to side, rang it. The ominous-sounding clapper struck the sides of the brasswork, sending out a melancholy, dull ring. He waited, listening, before ringing it again. And, after a further wait, again.

Bert opened the latch, swung the gate open and pushed the barrow along the winding path, senses alert for anyone's approach. On either side, tall trees pressed down on him, but nothing stirred amongst their black branches. No birds, animals, nothing. He pressed on, wondering how long the path might be. Sweat sprouted from his brow, his exertions with the barrow mingling with the mounting feeling of trepidation that accompanied every step. The first tingling of fatigue developed in his shoulders and forearms. Bert could run forever, but shoving this barrow along an ill-kept dirt track was not something he was used to.

Calling Josh every name he could think of, he moved on as the trees suddenly gave way to an open vista, stretching wide before him; ornamental gardens, laid out in a symmetrical pattern, with rectangular areas of flowers, roses mostly, surrounded by neatly trimmed box hedges. He allowed himself a grin of self-satisfaction and took in the impressively large house, with its many windows and large, heavy door approached by a set of broad, stone steps. What lay within its solid walls was anybody's guess, but Bert would put money on there being mountains of treasure, paintings, jewels. Spitting into his palms, he heaved the barrow to the foot of the steps, settled it down and walked up to the entrance.

Not pausing to congratulate himself for getting this far, Bert pulled at the doorbell and waited.

Seconds seemed to stretch on forever. He waited. Slowly he turned and looked back out across the well-tendered lawns. Set in the centre of the rose gardens, an ornate fountain captured most of his attention and he thought he saw little dancing fish playing within the spray. It would be nice to be a fish, he thought, especially one in that fountain, free from danger. Or simply just free. No more Rooster, no more orders, no more scraping and struggling. He gritted his teeth. When all was said and done, his life was meaningless and hard and one day he would end up like that old lady on the step of the shop. Forgotten. Alone. Dead, or soon to be so. He shuddered at the thought.

Then, from somewhere deep within the house, he heard the faint but definite sound of padding feet slowly approaching. Putting his daydreams aside, he hastily adjusted his necktie, straightened his cap and tucked in his shirt. He stood ramrod straight, a soldier on parade, and gave his best business-like smile.

The door opened.

A gnarled little old lady, wearing a black, high-collared, raised-waist-style dress, the full sleeves gathered in tight cuffs at her stick-thin wrists, stood in the doorway. She was stooped over like a vulture, her small head perched on the end of a thin, scraggly neck, her breathing percolated in her throat in a soft gurgle. A claw-like hand feebly gripped the edge of the door, her crinkled brow creasing into a deep, mistrusting frown as her watery, unblinking eyes studied Bert with obvious disapproval. She waited.

Bert shuddered. He had never liked old people, dead or alive. And this one was somewhere in-between. He knew it was silly, but he found old folk threatening, scary. Already he felt the fear pricking at the nape of his neck as this one ran her rheumy eyes over him. Forcing a smile, he swallowed hard. "Chimney swept, ma'am?"

The old lady's frown remained etched on her face. "Chimney?" Her voice, like her body, was feeble but carried an echo of an authority that she must have once possessed. "I have not asked for my chimneys to be swept."

Bert, well prepared as always for such a question, smiled broadly. "I understand that, ma'am, but as I made my way into town, I noticed this wonderful house from the road with all its many chimneys. So I presumed…"

"*Presumed*? You have a fair command of speech for one such as you!" She gave him a cursory glance from head to foot. "Have you ever attended school?"

Bert smiled again, proud of the answer he was about to give. "Sunday school, yes, ma'am."

"Well, that is something at least. You saw my house from the roadside, you say?"

"Yes ma'am. I was making my way from town –"

"You cannot see my house from the roadside."

Her words bit into Bert's face and he felt his cheeks burn. This old lady was not to be trifled with. She was as sharp as flint, that much was certain. Her fragile carapace hid a stern and resourceful nature. Fighting to keep down the growing sense of unease welling up inside him, he did his best to sound confused. "Did I say roadside?"

Her eyes narrowed, watching him, measuring him. "You did, indeed."

"I meant from the gate, ma'am. *The gate.* I rang the big bell there, ma'am. Just now. I was curious, you see. Thought I would –"

"You *presumed* – that is what you said?" She looked at him even more keenly, searching his face for the slightest sign of deceit, sucked in her breath and continued, "So, you presumed to come and offer your services? Is that it?" As she pursed her lips, a thin red tip of a tongue poked out between tiny, even teeth. "You also said *from* town, but previously you said you were going *into* town. Which is it?"

Bert's shoulders slumped. The old dear had seen right through him. If she could work him out this quickly, then perhaps old Rooster's idea about nicking the family china or the contents of a moneybox would also fall down flat. Rooster wouldn't like it. He'd said as much. "Now, Bert," he'd said, leaning his face so close that Bert could pick out every vein in the man's watery eyes, "when you get inside, be sharp. There's bound to be heirlooms, trinkets and the like. Get as much into your sack as you can, make your excuses, and leave. Leave the sweeping gear behind. That way, suspicion will not be aroused as you make your way through the streets of town." But suspicion *had* been aroused, and Bert hadn't even stepped inside yet.

"You'd better come in," she said briskly, and shuffled to one side to allow him to do so.

For a moment, Bert stood frozen to the spot, taken aback. He was in? After all she had said? He couldn't believe it.

"Well, come along," she snapped. "I'm not usually in the habit of letting complete strangers into my home, but you look as though you could do with the business. Come in."

Bert doffed his cap, sucked in a deep breath and boldly stepped inside.

Once in, he stood still and looked around him. The broad entrance hall was bright, the walls and ceilings stark white, with numerous paintings hanging from them in gilded frames. A large chandelier, suspended by a golden chain from a huge, decorative rose, sparkled high above him. It was like nothing he'd ever seen before.

He licked his lips. So far, so good. Now, all he had to do was make as if he were a skilled sweep and, before he could count to fifty, he would be out and on his way back to Rooster. At least, that was the idea. He just hoped that it would all work out the way Rooster wanted.

As things were to turn out, it didn't.

Chapter Five

'All That Glitters...'

Watching him like a hawk, she never let him out of her sight. Wherever he went, whatever he did, she was there, silently studying every move. Bert sensed those eyes boring into his back as he got down on his haunches in front of the main fireplace and wondered what he could do. The more time ticked by, the less likely it seemed that the opportunity for lifting anything, anything at all, would ever arise. So, to keep his mind off the hopelessness of it all, he forced himself to concentrate on the task in hand – sweeping the chimney. Or, to be more accurate, *pretending* to sweep the chimney, for Bert didn't have an inkling of how he should go about such a chore.

He made a brave show of going through the motions, appearing, or so he hoped, that he knew what he was doing. Firstly, he investigated the various chimneybreasts throughout the downstairs rooms, making great play of measuring them, stepping back, cocking his head to one side, tapping his chin. Back in their stinking, broken-down headquarters down by the river, Mr Rooster had insisted that he go through this charade time and time again until it became second nature and now here he was, trying every trick he knew to make his actions appear natural and unforced. From the sound of her heavy breathing, he wasn't too sure if he was succeeding.

Once he had chosen a 'suitable' fireplace, the next step called for him to quickly assemble the brushes and cover the various items of furniture with grey canvas sheets he kept in his holdall. Again, Rooster had helped prepare the young thief, endlessly rehearsing the process, which proved well-founded as the old lady, as alert as any predator, took careful note of every move he made. He tried a smile but, with no response forthcoming, he once more put all of his efforts into his preparations.

Despite his extremely impressive play-acting, he was not to be distracted from the real reason why he was there. All the time, he had one eye on what he was doing whilst the other scanned the room for things he could snatch. In that particular aspect, there was plenty he *could* snatch, given half the chance. Silver candlesticks, snuff-boxes, cigarette cases, ornaments, porcelain figurines, pictures, cutlery – every piece hallmarked, no doubt – bone china dinner services; everything the discerning thief could wish for was here, and all of it easily portable. Old Rooster would flip his lid if he could see all this, mused Bert. But then an impatient tapping of a foot brought him back to reality and he returned for a more concerted effort on the job in hand.

After some time, the old lady suddenly spoke. "Are you going to go up?"

Bert had made a meal of putting together the brushes, but the old lady was not to be fooled for much longer. They were standing in what Bert assumed to be the main dining room and the huge empty fireplace, flanked by white-marble pillars, seemed to be mocking him. Looking from the chimney-breast, then to her, he hoped she hadn't noticed the expression of horror on his face. The chimney was massive, the pristine marble glaring back at him, hard and unrelenting. Not unlike the old lady in many ways. Ancient and unshakeable. Its sheer size made it certain that someone as small as Josh could easily fit inside its gaping, cavernous grate. But Josh wasn't here and the thought that soon

Bert would have to force himself to scale up the inside of that sooty shaft terrified him. He'd heard all the stories, about small boys, often smaller than he was, becoming trapped in the tight, squeezing confines of chimney shafts... how they had remained there, dying from thirst or fear, or both. Many were never found again and the more he thought of these horrors, the more he found it difficult to move. Sweat broke out on his brow as the enormity of what he faced dawned on him. But no matter what his fears were, there was simply nothing else for it – he would have to climb up the shaft.

Setting down the long brush poles, he dusted off his hands before spitting into them. Ignoring the old woman's harsh expulsion of breath, he dipped under the mantelpiece and gazed up into the blackness. He wondered what he was doing all of this for. Surely there were better ways to make a living – dishonest or otherwise? Rooster always chose him for the dirtiest, most difficult of jobs. The old man said it was because Bert was his most trusted 'associate'. *Associate...* Now, there was a laugh – what sort of a word was that to use for someone who was virtually a slave? He may well be the best of Rooster's crew, but that didn't make things any easier to take. He really was little more than a slave; he had no choice, no say in anything and the only rewards he had gained since joining Rooster were a roof over his head and one decent meal a day. No riches, no fortunes, just endless jobs, which brought in little more than a few pennies, and this one would prove the same.

"Are you going to get up there or stand around gawping all day?"

He shot the old woman a glance, spat on his hands again, and forced his way upwards into the tight space of the chimney.

It proved hard going, with few handholds, the bricks slippery, caked in soot. Rooster promised him riches, but it was all nonsense, just like those shiny baubles down below. Stuck in this black, choking hellhole, everything he'd seen became nothing but worthless trinkets. Someone had duped Rooster into believing there was treasure locked away somewhere inside. The objects were fakes, all of them. This was going to be like every other job that had gone before – a complete waste of time and effort.

He cursed as he almost lost his grip, his palms scraping across the rough brickwork. With his back pressed hard against one side and his feet against the other, he painfully shuffled his way upwards like some rat in a drainpipe. He didn't dare look down. His whole concentration was fixed on one goal – to get to the top. Once he reached the roof, he would make his way back to the dockside hideout. Then he'd let Rooster know what he thought of him! Yes, he would do that, in no uncertain terms. Afterwards, he'd pack his bag and make his way to London. Rooster wouldn't be able to stop him, not this time. No more being told what to do, not for Bert. No, he'd make his own mark, find his fortune, have a good life in the sprawling capital city of England, the capital of the Empire. If he could just get to the end of this blinking chimney, he could...

His thoughts froze in his head.

He squeezed his eyes into slits as he tried to focus on what he thought he had just seen. He looked again and yes, there it was – a tiny ray of light trickling out from between the brickwork. It couldn't be from outside, he was facing the wrong way. No, this was an interior light. A bedroom perhaps, with a fireplace that shared the same chimney? He pressed one of the bricks with the toe of his boot and it ever so slightly slid inwards. Here was a chance, a chance to do good by Rooster and then get away from the house, perhaps down the back stairs, without meeting up with the old lady again. One loose brick meant there could be more and if he could make a big enough hole...

Manoeuvring around, he managed to bring his body close to the chink. He pressed the brick with his hand. It moved again, very easily. There appeared to be no mortar binding it to its close companions. He took in a breath then pushed the brick with as much force as he could muster without over-balancing himself. The brick fell inwards with a great clunk as it hit the floor, taking three or more of its friends along for the ride. Bert settled himself, careful not to slip, and pushed again, putting all his youthful strength into the action. A mass of the rotten bricks fell inwards, sending out bursts of pink dust. Without exerting much effort, he worked quickly now, as much of the mortar was either old and perished, or missing altogether. Before he knew it, he'd created a sizeable hole.

Bert twisted his body around and stuck his head into the gap. Frantically, hardly daring to breathe, he wriggled though and managed to force his way inside.

This was no bedroom.

Pressing his palms against the floor, he levered himself up and scanned his surroundings, taking in the details. The fact was, it wasn't a room at all, but more like a cramped, secret compartment, barely big enough for a grown adult to stand upright in. As he tentatively drew himself to his full height, his head grazed the roof, and he instinctively flinched. But, as his hand went to rub the spot where the bricks had torn his skin, he stopped and gawped at the sight before him.

A large chest, with wide metal bands wrapped around the body and strengthened at each corner, sat grim and black, like a slumbering monster waiting for a victim to approach too close. If opened, what horrors might be unleashed from within its mysterious belly? What horrible, slimy thing lurked in the confines of its interior? Would it be loathsome and slippery, would thick, oozing tentacles reach out and seize him and drag him down into a gaping, slavering mouth full of rotted teeth and venomous fangs? Bert's stomach turned to liquid, his knees growing weak. His mind whirled with confusion and indecision. He knew he should not open this thing, even if he could... But how could he not?

Above him, light flooded the room from a skylight set in the ceiling. Grateful for it but nevertheless curious, he wondered why anyone would build such a room? What was its purpose? What could be inside the chest that had forced persons unknown to hide it away in a place such as this? Whoever had brought it here must have laboured for hours, using pulleys or winches to haul the chest upwards in the narrow confines of the chimney, then bricked it up, presumably to return at some later date to… to do what? Share out the booty? Was it ill-gotten gains, the proceeds of a robbery? Why else go to all this effort to conceal whatever it was that awaited discovery inside?

Rubbing his chin, he studied the cracked leather surface. It was old, but well made. And when he gave a tentative shove with his boot, it proved heavy. Answers to his questions would have to wait – Bert's only interest was in what was in it.

With no padlock, it seemed to be pleading for him to open it, to look inside, to discover what kind of treasures had waited so long at the bottom of the chest to be found. Its invisible, hypnotic power reached out to him and he could not resist. Even if he had wanted to, the desire to open the chest proved overwhelming. He took a step towards the great box, put his hands under the lid, held his breath and heaved it open.

Gasping, he sprang back, the lid closing with a resounding slam.

It couldn't be, it had to be a trick of the light! He glanced at the skylight. No. No trick. He took another breath and heaved the lid open once more.

This time, with his heart pounding and his breath coming in short, sharp intakes, Bert allowed himself to take in every detail and, as he did, his eyes bulged so far he thought they might pop.

Inside the box was a great, glittering jumble of jewels, trinkets, coins and other precious objects, tossed inside together like the ingredients of some fantastic, and vastly expensive, stew. He fell to his knees, gazing down into the unbelievable mass of glittering gems. Running his tongue over his dried lips, he plunged his hand inside, allowing his fingers to explore the tangle of silver, gold and jewels, feeling their strangeness, their warmth. It was like nothing he had ever experienced before and when he brought up his hand and opened his fingers to allow the treasures to jingle back amongst the rest, he tipped back his head and burst into uncontrolled laughter. Here was a world of wealth and of riches, like nothing he, nor Rooster, nor anyone else in this good, fair city could possibly imagine – a passport to a new and better life. One without worries or fears. A world where all of his dreams could become reality.

All at once, a distant memory sparked off in his head, of a story told to him by his mother, about a thief who had stumbled upon a magical cave and discovered a wealth of treasure. Ali Baba! That was it, Ali Baba! "That's me," he said out loud, "I'm Ali Baba!"

He looked around anxiously, aware of how loud his voice sounded in that tiny room, and suddenly remembering where he was.

But there was no sign of anyone. Indeed, it seemed to him that nobody had set foot in this room since the day they bricked it in, whoever 'they' were.

He wiped his brow as the first beads of sweat broke out and dripped onto the floor. What to do, he pondered. There was no way he could pull out the chest. It was too big, too heavy. Perhaps, if Rooster could get a gang up here and – his fist came down into the palm of his other hand. He'd be damned if Rooster was going to get his grubby mitts on this lot! No, this was for him and for him alone.

Quickly, without any plan or thought, he stuffed his pockets with fistfuls of the fabulous hoard. When these were filled, he used the front of his shirt as a kind of carrier bag, tying up the sides to stow away just one more trinket...

Reluctantly, he closed the lid very quietly and slowly made his way back through the improvised entrance to the chimney. He looked back for one last time. Everything seemed the same. The great chest stood in exactly the same spot, giving no hint that it had been disturbed and plundered, despite the broken bricks spread all around. And yet something caught his attention, something different affecting the atmosphere, even causing the light above to change to a dull, threatening grey, unfriendly, even angry.

Shaking his head, he cleared away the growing feeling of unease, gave the bulges in his pockets a reassuring pat and grinned. Everything was as it should be and from this point on, life was going to be good. With a new resolve, he set to squeezing himself through the gap in the bricks. However, almost immediately, this proved not as easy as he had first envisaged. The gap seemed somehow narrower than it had been before, forcing him to struggle and strain to wriggle his body through. The rough surface of the bricks scraped at his knees and shins, and he groaned not only with his efforts, but at the growing number of cuts and grazes he suffered.

Twisting himself around, he managed to squeeze his upper body free. The blackness of the shaft disappeared beneath him. Craning his neck, he caught sight of a dull smudge of sky drifting across the chimney opening some way above him. He paused, battling to keep his breathing even, gripped the edge of the brickwork and pulled his legs through. For one sickening moment, his feet dangled into the abyss, but he held on fast, brought up his knees

and pushed out towards the opposite wall. Free of the room at last, he pressed his palms hard against the wall and continued his laborious and painful journey up towards the roof.

Chapter Six

Escape in the Dark

By now, it was late afternoon and Bert was in no mood to hang about. He knew that the old lady would be suspecting the worst and he wanted to put as much distance between himself and the house as he possibly could. So, ignoring the physical danger, once he had emerged through the chimney stack, black, dirty, wet with sweat, he took a moment to consider his situation. And from here, the situation appeared bleak.

On either side, the roof, divided into various sections of differing heights and angles, stretched dull grey, the slates shiny as if wet with rainwater. The surrounding gardens, with the tree-line beyond, appeared impossibly small. He was high above the ground, higher than he had thought and, as he took a first step and tottered along the roof apex, he realised that one slip might be his last. Getting down on hands and knees, he edged forward, but knew that at some point he must begin the dreadful descent.

Considering his options, which were few, he stopped and turned his eyes to the place where the roof slanted sharply downwards. Judging the distance, he settled himself onto his backside, took a breath and launched himself forwards, sliding down across the smooth surface, using the heels of his shoes as brakes, slowing down his descent. He was anxious not to topple over the edge of roof and find himself in free-fall. If that happened, he was so high up that he would probably fly to his death, so he jammed down hard with his heels. As he slid downwards, the edge loomed closer, the guttering beyond the slates in clear view. He would need to grab hold of the guttering and hope it would support his weight. There was no other choice but, as his mind raced faster than his descent, so instinct took over from considered reason. Reaching the end, his feet touched the guttering and he jabbed his shoe heels into it, whilst he flapped his arms around wildly, desperate to find a crack or a jutting-out piece of slate to cling onto. His fingertips brushed across something and he held on, straining every muscle and sinew to bring himself to a stop.

He had been lucky. Lying on his back, his left arm twisted impossibly behind him, and his feet wedged inside the guttering, he took a few moments to get his breath back and gather his thoughts. He groaned, twisting his upper body around, and somehow managed to flip himself over onto his stomach. Lying there, breath rasping from his heaving chest, he offered up a silent prayer of thanks before chancing a glance downward. He grinned in relief. He had indeed been fortunate. The roof he lay on gave way to another on a lower storey. A drop of only a few feet separated the two. Slowly, he released his hold and flicked his feet up, freeing them from the gutter. Instantly, his descent resumed. With less than a foot to go before he reached the edge, he was suddenly clear and landed heavily, but without injury, on his backside. He climbed to his feet and, moving like a high-wire performer with arms stretched out wide for balance, he edged his way to what he hoped was a safe area and, finding one, jumped down onto the grass some twelve feet or so beneath.

Without a pause to catch his breath, he broke into a run, skirting around the house to the front. Then, never looking back, he headed for the wooded area from which he first spied the house. After a few minutes, he made it to the first line of towering trees and crouched down, peering back at the house. He waited, but there was nothing. The old woman probably thought he was stuck in the shaft and was even now shouting up to him, asking if he was all right. What she would do when she discovered the truth, he had no idea. He got to his feet, his wheelbarrow forgotten, his only thought to get away. To run like the wind, back to the town-centre, to find Rooster and to hand over the treasure.

He was near the edge of town when he stopped abruptly. A developing thought, which had percolated away in his mind since he came across the treasure chest, took a more definite shape. It was a thought that only a few weeks ago he would never have dared consider. But now, things were different. Quite by accident, he had stumbled upon the key to a better life. Why *should* he give Rooster the treasure? After all, what had he ever done for Bert? Given him a roof over his head? Was that it, the sum total of his rewards for all he had done for that miserable, grasping, cantankerous old miser? When Bert thought of the endless bowls of greasy soup, the flea-infested blankets in which he was forced to sleep, the cold, the damp, the constant fear of being caught by the authorities… it was a nightmare existence, in all honesty. Here, jingling around in his pockets, was a way to escape from the life of drudgery and poverty to which he had been condemned. All he needed to do was go into town, find a pawnbroker and get as good a price as he could for the jewels.

As he thought about it, his fingers curled around the bunch of coins and jewels in his right trouser pocket. What could it all be worth, he wondered? More than five pounds, that was for sure. Maybe twenty… fifty! His heart banged hard in his chest at the prospect of what it could all mean. Once he sold them, everything would be fine.

Or would it?

Rooster would find him eventually, and that would be that. He'd be dead, his throat cut and his body dumped in the river. Rooster may not get the money, but he'd get his revenge. Rooster was a man who knew everybody and everything. He had contacts everywhere. How long would it be before one of his informers spotted Bert and gave him up? Rooster had a reputation to maintain; he couldn't afford to be soft or unforgiving. In his line of business, there was only one consequence to disloyalty. Bert touched his throat, his imagination conjuring up a nightmare vision of a dark alleyway, rough hands grabbing him, the cold, sharp blade pressing against his skin...

He stifled a cry and quickly looked about him. No one noticed. People wandered by, lost in their own type of despair, sallow faces turned downwards to the filthy pavements. No one gave him a second glance. He wiped his forehead, and went to move on, but stopped.

Unless...

The solution, obvious in its simplicity, caused Bert to smile. Once he had the money, he could buy himself a train ticket to London. Rooster would never find him there. The old Cock-bird might be big in this northern city, but London? No, there he would be as insignificant as... well, as insignificant as Bert himself was right at that moment. A nothing, a nobody, invisible and uncared for. All he need do was act quickly.

As he thought through his plan, Bert wandered aimlessly through the busy streets of the town. People were everywhere, the busy bustle of the late afternoon creating a world of noise that was almost deafening. With his head down, ticking off a mental list of what he must do, he bumped into someone. The shock and power of the collision sent Bert reeling backwards. He stumbled and fell, landing awkwardly on his hip. He yelped, more in surprise than pain. A man, wearing a great, billowing overcoat with a bowler hat perched on top of his round, reddish face, loomed large over him. But he was kindly and he had been in a rush. As passers-by stopped to look, the stranger stooped down and helped Bert to his feet, concerned that the little lad might be badly hurt.

And then it happened.

As Bert stood up, thanking the man for his kindness, some of the jewels, dislodged no doubt by his jump from the roof, spilled out of his pocket and fell to the ground.

For an instant there was stunned silence. It seemed as if the whole world had suddenly come to a grinding halt and all eyes were turned on him.

The man was the first to recover. Bending down, he picked up one of the sparkling items and eyed it with awe. It was a heavy gold bracelet, and he weighed it in his hand. Those same round eyes now turned to Bert, bulging with questions. Then, across his face, came a dawning realisation. Bert, instinctively acting on Rooster's training, whirled away and was already careering down the street as what sounded like a hundred voices raised up to shout those fearful words, "STOP THIEF!"

* * *

Bert didn't know how far he had run when eventually he threw himself over a high brick wall and landed heavily on the ground on the other side. Pressing himself up against the bricks, mouth open, gulping down air, he remained as still as he could still, listening out for the sound of the approaching crowd. But there was nothing, not even the dreadful, piercing shrill of a policeman's whistle. Cautiously, he raised himself up to his full height, checked his pockets to make sure none of the other gems had fallen out, and looked around.

He stood in an old backyard, dark and miserable, with nothing growing except for a few lonely weeds sprouting between the cracks in the cobbled ground. Shrouded in a weak and gloomy light, the far corners were in darkness, but around him Bert managed to pick out a sea of broken, brittle bricks, old bits of furniture and rotting garbage littering the ground. A rubbish tip, or a dumping ground. Once again, luck was with him, for he could so easily have landed into a mangled mass of rusted metal, gashed his leg or, worse still, broken an ankle.

Across the heap of forgotten waste, a dark, silent house, obviously deserted, with the windows smashed in, waited as if mocking him, laughing at his plight. This old slum dwelling, typical of the kind of rundown property found everywhere throughout the town, its blackened walls looking as if they would crumble at any moment, offered his only means of shelter. It was the sort of place Bert knew well, having been born and raised in an identical house, growing up with the stench of damp clinging to every inch of him, the constant hunger gnawing away inside. A picture, a long-forgotten image, came to him, of his mother standing at a sink, crying, while his father lay slumped in a threadbare chair, snoring loudly, the empty gin bottle rolling noisily by his side. His brother, just a bundle in the corner, swathed in filthy rags, his sister crouched on the ground, her huge, dark eyes peering out of an ashen, sunken face. All of them struggling to survive in the misery, the hopelessness of a world that didn't care.

Shaking away the images, and with the gloom deepening, he picked his way through the detritus of the years and slammed into the solid trunk of a great tree. Cursing, he rubbed his face where the hard bark had struck him, and peered up into the tangle of branches. Although he was shocked that he hadn't noticed the tree before, its presence brought him some level of comfort. Undoubtedly older than the house, it nevertheless appeared to be in much better condition, healthy, solid and dependable. It would make a perfect lookout place from where he could spot any pursuers. So, spitting into both palms, he reached for the closest branch and hauled himself upwards. Within seconds, he reached the first of the more substantial branches, the climb proving infinitely easier than his ascent inside the chimney and very soon, he was in a good enough position to view the surrounding area.

Using the thicker of the branches for support, he found himself a safe, if uncomfortable place in which to sit. Hard, knotted lumps and sharp spikes dug into his flesh, but he had no choice other than to sit and wait. If he wriggled around too much, he might fall and land amongst the foul, stinking clutter below. Even worse, he could attract unwanted attention from any pursuers close by. He would just have to grit his teeth and bear it.

So, resigned, he settled between the fork of two sturdy branches. Evening drew in but he wasn't safe yet. Occasionally, the sound of voices, some close by, some more distant, drifted up to his perch, so, controlling his breathing, he forced himself to be still. Time crawled by, but each passing second brought with it a growing sense of relief. No one would pay much attention to an old tree, or the boy nesting amongst its branches. His pounding heart calmed and as he sat hunched up, exhaustion slowly enveloped him and soon, all troubles forgotten, he slipped into sleep.

Chapter Seven

Home Again

Awake...

It was daylight and he was freezing cold. Jamie rolled over, pulling the deep-piled quilt up to his neck, snuggling down into the soft and reassuring depths, a contented smile crossing his face.

His eyes snapped open.

For one wonderful moment, he had supposed he was back in his own bed, safe and sound. But now the truth dawned and the memories came flooding back. He was still there. In that house. Minutes passed. He lay as still as he could, listening out for any sound, any hint that the owners had returned. But there was nothing, only the thumping of his own heart, sounding louder to him than a bass drum.

A sudden resolve seized him. His poor mother would be worried out of her mind. Perhaps she had already notified the police. He threw back the covers and swung his legs out of the bed. He crossed the room at a run and tore at the door, then sprinted along the hallway, heading frantically, almost blindly, for the staircase and home, his missing friend completely forgotten. If Jamie had stopped to think, he may well have begun a further search for Tim, but all he cared about right now was getting away, far away from this awful house and never coming back.

The hallway flashed by as he ran, head down, relying on intuition alone to take him back to the front door. He had no idea of time, only a burning desire to escape. He took the stairs two at a time until, at last, he was there at the main at the entrance, and he stepped out into the fresh air. Slamming the great door behind him, he straddled his bike and made for the wooded entrance as quickly as he could, legs pumping away at the pedals at a frantic pace. Gritting his teeth, he steered himself across the thick, uncared-for grass, the dew soaking his trainers. His eyes scanned the sprawling grounds. The morning light bathed them in a comforting glow, making the surroundings seem benign, welcoming almost. Jamie scowled at the thought, knowing what lay within the walls, that inside the house was a malignancy which had enticed and then ensnared him. Tearing his eyes towards the trees, he increased his exertions.

Squealing brakes brought him to a halt by the main gate. Traffic trundled past. It seemed like early morning rush hour. Lucky people going about their normal, daily work. How he wished he were one of them; indeed, how he wished he was *anyone* except himself.

Nothing in the whole history of the world could be as terrible as this. Again, his mind turned to his mum and her face, imagining tears replacing the anger she must have initially felt when he didn't come home for tea. Probably the police were there even now, making their notes, sending out the patrols. Yet the Peelers wouldn't know where to look. If only he had...

His thoughts ground to a halt.

"*Peelers?*" he asked out loud to no one in particular. Where had that word come from? A slow smile worked its way across his face as the remnants of what happened gradually came into focus. Of course – the dream. The details came back to him, slowly at first, then in a great rush. Bert, the chimney, the jewels, the chase down the street, all of it so vivid. Not like a dream at all, really. More like a film... or a memory?

Jamie shuddered.

It was that house. Ghosts from the past making his imagination work overtime. He turned and looked back. That house... Could there really be hidden treasures still inside, locked away and forgotten in that tiny secret room high up in the chimney? Another shudder ran through him as he thought of the interior, the room in which he'd slept so soundly. And Tim. What about Tim?

Putting his head down, he rode out into the traffic, heading for home.

As he cycled, a single idea took root in his mind. It was an idea that was at once terrifying yet at the same time strangely seductive.

He could go back.

Not only find Tim, but climb the chimney for himself.

Discover the truth...

* * *

Some hours later, he sat alone on the floor of his room, back against his bed, staring at the walls. Downstairs, he could hear Mum's voice, shouting down the telephone. Sometime during last night, she had told Dad and now they were fighting about it. Probably Dad was telling her not to be so uptight, to take it easy, not be too hard on Jamie. But Mum wasn't listening. Mum never listened. After he'd thrown his bike into the back garden shed and rolled into the house, she'd stood in the kitchen, frozen in the act of washing dishes when she saw him, her black-rimmed eyes bulging, her mouth hanging open. Then, the reaction. At first, overcome by relief, she had thrown her arms around him, repeatedly kissing his face, almost taking his breath away. Perhaps it wasn't going to be all that bad after all, he thought. But within an instant, everything had changed. The shouting, the shaking, her face twisted into a mask of fury. "Why didn't you phone me?" He showed her his mobile, the battery drained. "What is the point in having it if you can't bloody well use it?" She seethed, shoulders rising and falling. "Do you want to kill me, is that what you want?" It was all so awful – the worst ever! Within moments, she sent him to his room, ordering him to stay there until... until...

Swallowing hard, Jamie pressed both fists into his eyes, wishing this nightmare away. But it wasn't going to go away. The police would be here soon, to give him a good telling-off. Worse than anything that could happen at school. God, why had he been so stupid? Why hadn't he stood up to Tim and said, "No, I'm going home!"

Tim.

In all the upset, Jamie had almost forgotten about his friend, still lost within that dreadful house. He'd made no mention of his friend, knowing full well what his mother's reaction would be if she knew Tim was in some way involved. She disliked Tim intensely, considering him to be a 'bad influence', not understanding that Tim was the only friend he had. If he could keep Tim's name out of this, then perhaps things wouldn't be so bad.

He dragged his hands down and stared wildly at the blank walls in front of him. Why was he protecting Tim, even now? Why couldn't he just tell his mum the truth and face the consequences? What else could happen? He'd already been grounded. If Tim's name came out, then what would be the outcome? Would he be banned from ever seeing him again? Perhaps, in light of everything that had happened, that wouldn't be such a bad thing.

Pressing his face into his hands, Jamie let out a prolonged, despairing groan.

No, that could never be. For all Tim's faults, he really was Jamie's only friend. Jamie, the class swot. Top of his year in maths and English. Even better than Sarah Jarvis, and everyone hated Sarah Jarvis. God, to be a *boy* and to be so *good*, it wasn't fair! Tim was the only one who seemed to have any time for him. He recalled how, on his first day at the new school, Tim had marched across the playground, offered him some crisps and invited him round to play a game of football.

At first, Jamie had refused, thinking it was some awful practical joke. Nobody *ever* spoke to him. And a new boy? But then, some days later, Tim called at his house, standing there in the porch, bouncing a football, smiling. A friend. Mum had said it would be okay to go out and play. So he'd gone and he'd had the best night of his life, just kicking a football around, practising penalty kicks. But what made it so memorable was Tim. Tim accepting him for who he was. They'd laughed so much, Jamie thought his chest would explode. A friend. A true friend.

Of course, some weeks later, he discovered the reasons. Tim, too, had problems. He was tough. Hard. His temper was well known throughout the school. Short, wiry, fists always ready to swing into action, even the older boys were wary of him. How many fights had Jamie witnessed, Tim pummelling his opponents into a bloody mess, the shrieks, the pleading for him to stop? He never did. Everyone feared him. No one called him 'friend'.

Except Jamie.

Two opposites. Jamie, so meek, so quiet. Tim, brutal, unforgiving. Pushed away, shunned by the rest, the two boys gravitated towards one another and found a sense of comfort and acceptance in their shared company.

Jamie let out a deep, mournful moan. Oh, why couldn't *last* night have been just another ordinary night of football and laughter, instead of all this trouble?

He quietly wept into his hands as despair overcame him. He didn't know what to do. Tell the truth, lose his friend?

And if he didn't tell?

His great enemy, his inability to make decisions, had come to haunt him once more. What had got him into this whole, dreadful mess in the first place, was now making his life miserable once again. If only he had the strength to simply stand up and do the right thing – speak out the truth

Dragging his hands away, he sniffed loudly and stared out of his window. A dreadful realisation dawned. A thought he had not considered since waking up in that horrible room so many hours ago. What if Tim truly was lost, trapped in that awful house, shivering, cold and lonely in some dark, dank cellar?

"*Mum!*" he shouted, resolved at last to do something, to face whatever the consequences might be. Tim was worth more than this.

He tore open his bedroom door and collided with the ample midriff of a very large man.

Jamie looked up.

The policeman didn't smile.

* * *

The interrogation proved ghastly, with no mercy shown. The good thing was, Jamie had told the truth, the correct decision because the police knew it all anyway. They'd found Tim. Trembling like a little lost animal, he mumbled on about ghosts and shadows and a big bird that was going to come and take him away. The police had gone to the house in answer to a telephone call from somebody who had seen Jamie emerging from the gateway earlier that morning. The description of the missing boys had been circulated to local newspapers, radio and television. People don't miss a trick, not if they know it's important, he thought. This person had put the two events together and told the police, and thank God for it, mused Jamie, for without them being so observant and public-spirited, Tim could still be there, locked away with only his nightmarish thoughts for company.

Jamie shivered. If only he could see his friend, get a message to him, anything, just to let him know, make him understand that he had become lost... that he had never meant to abandon him. This thought, above everything else, ate away at him – that his only real, true friend might think that he, Jamie, had simply left him there, all alone, in that great, big house. But Mum, as had been expected, had said that he could never see Tim again. And Tim's mum, contacting them as soon as her son had returned safe, if not traumatised, had said much the same thing. So that was that. No more friends, and three more weeks of the holiday still to go and nobody to share it with.

"Sarah's coming round for tea," Mum told him, closing the door softly behind the policeman when he left. "Day after to-morrow, that is. As for the rest of today, and every other day until you go back to school, you are grounded from seeing any-one else. I'll not have any more of this nonsense, do you understand me?"

"Yes, Mum, I understand." But Mum... *Sarah Jarvis*? What are you thinking!

Jamie fell back on his bed and closed his eyes, wishing it all away. She'd invited herself to his house ages ago. He'd tried to put her off, knowing what everyone else would think and say... especially Tim. But there was no dissuading Sarah. She'd even gone so far as to talk to Mum over the phone. "Sounds like a nice little girl," Mum had said. Yeah. Very nice.

He turned over and stared at the posters on his wall. His mum had let him put up *The Terminator* film posters after a great deal of pleading and promises that he'd do all his weekly jobs on time, without complaint. He'd bought them at the Cinema Shop in London, costing all his savings, but they were original and worth every penny. Some time back, Dad had bought him an original German version of *A Fistful of Dollars*, which now hung proudly next to the others. Such collectibles were an important part of his life. A private part of his life.

What would she think of them? Sarah Jarvis?

Sarah was the name of the girl in the *Terminator* films. Sarah Connor.

Jamie closed his eyes. Truth be known, if he allowed himself to be honest, Sarah Jarvis was quite nice. Everyone hated her because she was so clever, but all the boys fancied her like mad. Gorgeous honey-blonde hair, enormous green eyes set in a face which belonged on the cover of a magazine. Such a face! And now she was coming to tea, to his house. The stuff that dreams were made of. Smiling to himself, and forgetting all about his inner conflict over Tim, Jamie wallowed in the glorious warm feeling spreading out from his tummy. Perhaps things were going to turn out for the best, after all? Bringing up his knees, he curled himself up into a ball of blissful anticipation, yawned, and drifted into sleep.

Chapter Eight

Annabel

Dreaming…

Bert woke up, startled and afraid. The night pressed in coal black from all sides and for one terrible moment, he completely forgot where he was. With panic gripping him, he wrenched himself over onto his side. With a sudden sharp splintering of wood, his precarious perch gave way and he fell through empty space to land heavily on the ground below. The force of the impact left him breathless, bruised and dazed but otherwise uninjured.

Flailing out with his arms to dash away a legion of demons, he scrambled to his feet, a blind man lost in a strange place. As he stood there rigid with fear, tears came rolling down his grimy cheeks, tears of confusion mixed with mounting terror. This place, wherever it was, offered no sanctuary, no possibility for giving him the means to regain his strength, or his wits. He was close to the end of his reason and there was nothing he could do.

Fearful he may have lost the jewels, he checked his coat and sighed with relief when his hand closed over the reassuring bulge in his pocket. He could not, however, dispel the dread of this place. And then, trickling out of the darkness, emerged a voice, soft and comforting, to chase away those demons. A girl's voice. "Don't be afraid," it said. Its tone seemed gentle and reassuring, but nevertheless Bert froze. He was afraid. A dim recollection of where he was and what had brought him here slowly parted the mist shrouding his mind. Who had spoken? The first of a gang of pursuers? He desperately wanted to run, to flee, to put as much distance from himself and this place as he could, but none of his limbs would work. It was as if his body had set solid. He could do nothing – except wait.

A bright light flared up and Bert watched bewitched as the owner of the voice revealed herself, setting a match to the wick of an oil lamp. Delicately, she replaced the glass bowl and, through the eerie orange glow, he made out her shadowy figure. Small and fragile-looking, she wore a long dress with a high-bodice, the kind only the well-to-do could afford, he thought. Other than that, any other details were too difficult to make out in the deep shadows cast by the lamp. Only her voice remained constant, hypnotising him with its gentleness, melting away his fear, causing his body to relax.

She stepped out of the shadows and he could see her more clearly. Indeed, she was elegantly dressed, but it was not this which held his attention, nor the blonde ringlets cascading down to below her shoulders, but her full, bright eyes. Eyes so big he felt he could dive into them and lose himself inside there forever.

"My name is Annabel," she said softly. "This is my house. My tree. I was out here watching the stars when you fell out of it. For a moment, I thought you had fallen from the sky." She gave a little giggle. "That would have been silly, but I'm so full of fairy-stories that I almost wished you had." She stepped closer still, studying him from top to toe with a measured look. "You did frighten me, but I can see that you are the one who is frightened. Please don't be, I mean you no harm. Are you a workhouse boy, a runaway?"

Bert stood, listening to every word, feeling more and more soothed with each one. As he listened, his self-confidence returned and he at last found the power of speech. "No," he answered, "no, I'm not a runaway. I was chased by some people who thought I had done something that I had not. I hid until they had passed. I think I fell asleep."

"You think? Don't you know?"

"I suppose I must have done. I'm not in the habit of jumping out of trees and nearly breaking both my legs."

She studied him again for a long moment, holding the lamp higher to gain a better view. "You look terribly dirty. Would you like to come indoors? We have a bath and –"

"No," Bert blurted quickly, "that's quite all right, miss. I'll be on my way if you don't mind."

"Oh, but I *do* mind," she said, a strange, mocking tone in her voice. "You have to tell me all about yourself, why you were chased and where you live. If we were to talk out here, the Peelers might come and that is something I believe you would not wish to happen."

Bert's eyes grew round. "You'll not call them, miss?"

"No," she replied, with a disarming smile, "but they may come, notwithstanding. These buildings are a notorious meeting-place for thieves. All we can do is make the most of what we have." She smiled and took him by the hand. "Come inside."

Bert's eyes fell to her delicate fingers, the coolness of her touch sending a thrill through his body. Unable to resist, he allowed himself to be led into the crumbling building.

* * *

The house was dark and dank, draped in a heavy atmosphere of decay and neglect. Annabel apparently lived in the basement of the building, rooms she said she shared with her brother, their mother and another family. Bert was reluctant to believe this, as there was little evidence of anybody else ever having lived there. He could see only a few sticks of rickety furniture, a moth-eaten mattress for a bed and some tiny pieces of crockery stacked neatly upon the top of a worm-riddled cabinet. No other person was there, nor had anyone shared the cramped confines of the place for a long time, if ever. Perhaps, he began to suspect, it was *she* who was the runaway.

Bert sat at a creaking table and waited. Leaving the lamp beside him, Annabel slipped away into the gloom and returned after a few, brief moments with a steaming bowl of broth and set it down before him together with a large spoon. Not needing any encouragement, he hungrily attacked this offering, gobbling down every delicious mouthful without even a 'thank-you'. When he had finished, he threw down the spoon and cleaned the bowl with the hunk of bread she had supplied. He then sat back, licking his lips, feeling much better. All the time, in the lamp's glow, she watched him. Behind her, the weak, insipid light cast curious and grotesque shadows across the cracked walls, but nothing about this place caused him any fear now. This strange little girl, with her fancy clothes and her enormous eyes, dispelled any demons there might have been. He smiled and she smiled back.

What an adventure he had had, he thought to himself. Old Cock-bird and Josh may well laugh about all of this when they all finally met up again. *If* they ever did, he corrected himself, because he seriously doubted they ever would. Convinced Josh had been arrested, Bert knew what Rooster's reaction would be. Indeed, there was no telling the limits of what that horrible man might do when all of this reached its conclusion. Rooster was capable of anything. One thing was for sure, laugh he certainly would not. Bert knew that whatever the outcome, it would be more terrible than he could ever imagine.

All of this reinforced his decision that they should never met up again. Not with Josh, certainly not with Rooster. Besides, he now had his fortune, so the idea of escape was more realistic and achievable than ever before. He touched his pocket, to reassure himself that at least some of the treasure was still there. Allowing himself a smile as his fingers traced the shape of the bulging gems and coins, he sat back and licked his lips, contented.

Her unblinking, penetrating gaze never left him. It was as if she could read his thoughts, or was lost in her own, wondering who he was and what had brought him here. Tilting his head, he studied her under his brows. "Why do you live all alone here?" he said, his voice challenging.

The sudden question seemed to catch her off-guard. "I don't," she blurted out defensively and sat up, dusting away imaginary crumbs from her dress.

She wasn't convincing and Bert snorted. "Where is everyone else then?"

Annabel frowned, face reddening, growing angry. "You're much braver now that you've been fed."

Bert didn't want this reaction. She had helped him, and he was grateful. He leaned forward and made to touch her hand. She pulled hers away quickly.

"I'm sorry," he said, much more gently, "but it's so obvious, miss."

She looked at him sharply, another challenge already forming on her lips, but this brief moment of anger soon passed and her face softened again. Sighing deeply, she turned away from his gaze. "I didn't think I could fool you for long," she confessed. "I'll tell you my own little story, if you're interested."

"I am, miss," he said gently, sensing this was going to prove difficult for her. This time, when his hand crept across the table to take hers, she did not flinch.

"I was orphaned at an early age, and they took me away to the workhouse. Two men and a woman. The woman I'll never forget, her black eyes, so narrow, full of contempt and loathing.

She'd seen a hundred like me before and any compassion she felt was long gone."

"Miss," he said quickly, "I don't understand these big words. I'm sorry."

A smile. Warm this time. "She blamed me," she said. "As if it were my fault that my mother was dead! My brothers ran away, you see, leaving my mother alone in the house, growing weaker with each passing day. Father, well... I never knew my father. I have always hoped that one of my brothers was kind enough to go to the Guardians and tell them of my plight. Whatever or whoever told them, they came and they took me away.

"I grew up in there, in the workhouse, until recently. Life there was so miserable that when I was old enough, I decided life outside had to be better. Waiting for the right moment, I took my chance, hiding in the back of the local bakery van that delivered bread every week, same time, same day, like clockwork. Burying myself deep down amongst the bags of bread rolls, I made my escape. That was almost eight days ago, but I know for sure the authorities will be looking for me. My plan was to stay here in the basement of this house for another week at least, then slip on board a ferry and make my way across to Liverpool and, hopefully, get into domestic service there. I have no illusions as to how difficult such a course will be, but I'm determined to try. Anything is better than the Birkenhead Union Workhouse."

Bert agreed with that last part whole-heartedly. Rooster had told him many times about how hard and cruel it was inside the place. Red-bricked, high-vaulted corridors roamed through a dark and eerie world, soulless and uncaring – a world where matrons beat small boys into submission. Absolute obedience to the rules was demanded at all times. Anything less would result in instant punishment; punishment of the most extreme kind. It was an existence that was far more unforgiving than anything that could be found outside its stark and sinister walls. Cold. Desolate. Alone. Bert, utterly convinced by the stories he'd been told, had decided there and then that the only real alternative was turning to a life of crime.

"That place scares me, miss. Scares me worse than… well, death itself! So that's why I do what I do." He stared into those huge, kind eyes. "It's what I am, you see, miss. I'm a thief."

This revelation brought no reaction, not so much as a blink. "And that was why you were in the tree – you'd stolen something and the owners were trying to catch you."

Without thinking, he plunged his hands into his pockets and spread the treasure trove he had managed to hold onto across the table. He waited breathlessly for her reaction. What she did was smile.

Chapter Nine

Offers to Refuse

They slept amongst the debris, Bert feeling a lot more relaxed with Annabel so close, so trusting. He had told her everything, and she had listened without judging. She'd made some suggestions, devised some plans, and then it was time to sleep. Once or twice they were disturbed by the shuffling of rats, but both of them were well used to that and neither of them stirred. When morning came, they rose without discomfort and finished off the last of the bread. They then resolved to put their plan into operation. This little slip of a girl had convinced him of what he had to do. Her angelic face had captured his heart and he found he had neither the strength nor the desire to argue with her. Whatever she said was going to be fine by him. He trusted her without question.

This was a strange new experience for Bert. Up until now, he had always thought of girls as being prim and powdered things, with little to say except 'thank you, mum' and 'if you please, mum'. He knew better now. Annabel was unlike anyone – boy or girl – he had ever met. He was captivated by her loveliness. Her inner toughness was a thing to be admired. She had seen and done such a lot in her short life, this little girl, learning to survive on her wits. Intelligent and beautiful – an intoxicating combination!

Annabel, Annabel… He found himself repeating her name over and over in his mind. The thought of it was so lovely. Just like her. If only he could find the courage to tell her exactly how he –

"Bert!" came a voice, shattering his daydreaming. "Bert, are you with us today?"

Blinking, Bert looked up to see her big eyes smiling at him. He shook his head, clearing his thoughts. "Yes, yes, sorry about that." He smiled his apology, before he noticed the remnants of her own smile were now being replaced by a thin, hard line. A tight ball tightened in his guts. "What is it? What's wrong?"

Standing with hands on hips, she slowly shook her head, displeasure written across every feature. She let out a long sigh. "Don't you remember what we talked about last night?"

"I, er, yes, I *think* so."

"You think so?" She squatted down next to him. "The pawnbrokers? After you showed me the jewels, we talked about what we should do." She took his hand in hers and held it, patting it like a kindly schoolteacher would do to a confused child. "Please pay attention, Bert."

The smile returned, and he felt a little more at ease. If there was one thing he didn't want to do, *never* wanted to do, it was to displease her. So he listened attentively, his eyes never leaving hers. "We must find a pawnbroker and get what we can for them. But we must get as good a price as possible, so that might mean visiting more than one. We must be careful." She squeezed his hand, giving her words greater emphasis. "We must always keep to the side streets and be prepared to run fast if we have to. Remember the story we agreed upon if either of us gets caught?"

"Yes." He closed his eyes and saw the rehearsed words in his mind's eye. "We found the gems in the street, just off the Square."

Pushing her finger through the pile of jewellery, she picked up the ring, the one gem that had really taken her eye. Even in the dim light of the basement, it sparkled with its own inner beauty. Encrusted though it was with diamonds, it was the simple band of gold that drew most of her attention. Running along the inside of the band were inscribed the words: *My heart and soul are yours, forever.*

"I wonder who it was?" she thought out loud.

"Who what was?" asked Bert.

"The person who had these words inscribed on this ring. Written for that old lady in the house, no doubt, but by whom?"

Bert shrugged his shoulders. "An old admirer, perhaps. Or husband. How old do you think it is?"

"I don't know, that's for the pawnbroker to tell us. Valuable though, I should think."

"Is it?" Bert perked up at that. "What, worth a lot, you mean?"

"It must be. Look at all these diamonds." She thought for a moment. "It might be wiser if we didn't take everything to a single pawnbroker. Best if we split it into several lots. That way, no one will get too suspicious."

"Yes, you're right." Bert produced more of the gemstones and coins from his pockets to join the rest of the collection. "I think I must have dropped some of it, perhaps when I jumped from the roof, or bumped into that gentleman. I picked up more than this from the house, I'm sure."

Amongst the many coins, there were several more rings, some brooches, a bracelet and a very heavy necklace that seemed to be made from gold rope. Annabel tenderly hefted it in her fingers and sighed.

For several long moments, they both sat staring in silent awe at the glittering array, each embroiled in their own dreams, realising that here were the keys to another, better life. For Bert, he did not consider for a moment the morality of what had happened, or what they were planning on doing. That these were stolen goods, someone else's possessions, treasured and coveted so much that they had been stored away safe and sound, meant nothing to him. Hardened by a lifetime of thievery and dishonesty, taking such bounty was as natural to Bert as breathing. They had here the opportunity to end their miserable existence – an existence that saw them living by chance, scraping out a living from the dregs of society, no one caring for them, worrying about them or, most importantly, loving them. That world, if it had ever existed, was gone, lost in the tracks of time. Now, they only had themselves to worry about and, although they were young, they both knew enough to understand that life could be better. So what if the jewels were not theirs? Better to use them to start a new life than for them to remain all forgotten in that chest. What possible good was that? Any feelings of guilt and conscience could come later, when they were rich.

"It's not wrong, what we're going to do," he said quietly, conscious that Annabel, although clever and resourceful, was not a child of the streets like himself. "These jewels, they were made to be treasured, to be adored by their owner – whoever the owner might be. And these," he picked up a gold coin, turning it around in his fingers, "these were not made to be stowed away in some big box. They were meant to be spent. And we will spend them. You and me, Annabel."

"You're right. Of course you are." And she leaned forward and squeezed his hand. For a long time they sat like that, lost in their dreams once again.

Later, as if by some unspoken signal, they both stood up and gathered together a few meagre belongings. Annabel took a blanket and a small canvas bag, into which Bert placed just over half of the jewels. The rest he left in his pockets. "Better to spread them out," he explained, and they tramped along the hallway to the front door and stepped outside.

* * *

The morning that greeted them was grey and overcast, doing nothing to help raise their spirits. For a moment, they both stood, staring up at the leaden sky. Perhaps, by the end of the day, the sun would shine – at least, if not in the weather, then in their hearts.

"We're doing the right thing," he said, taking her by the hand.

"I know," she said, smiling.

The silence of the narrow street pressed in around them, heavy and depressing. Not even the cheeping of a sparrow relieved the tension which seemed to emanate from the row of dead, blackened houses on either side of the cobbles. "Let's go to town," said Bert and gently led her away from that sorrowful place towards the heaving bustle of Hamilton Square.

By the time they reached the city, the day was already clearer, patches of blue breaking up the uniform grey of the sky. The prospect of what lay before them lifted their spirits somewhat, despite their nervousness. Pawnbrokers were notorious for their guile, always giving the lowest possible rates. Many were considered dangerous, as indeed all types of moneylenders were. Their profession allowed them to be nothing less. As they walked, they gripped one another's hand hard.

The town centre heaved with people bustling to and fro. Noise came from everywhere. Street hawkers and vendors shouted out their wares, newspaper boys trilled their news. Carriages of every imaginable size trundled by, horses whinnying, iron-banded wheels making a tremendous din as they clattered along the cobbled streets. Trolley buses clanged their bells, whilst hansom cabs weaved in and out, picking up passengers who skipped and darted between the many vehicles. The air was full of the sound of industry and speculation. It was a mad, chaotic world and Bert loved every bit of it. This was his domain, the one in which he thrived, every new day presenting a host of different challenges and ways of pitting his wits against those of everyone else. Most importantly of course, he could pit himself against the authorities – and beating them was, for Bert, the most wonderful feeling of all.

The voice which penetrated the racket of the street had the effect of almost knocking him over, so great was the sense of shock it created in him. Alarmed, Annabel gripped his arm, raising her face to his, eyes questioning, lips trembling. Bert tried to offer her a smile of reassurance, but none came. This was not the time for reassurance. This was a moment of terror.

They both stood and stared as the owner of the voice emerged from the press of people, a small, bedraggled boy elbowing his way through, ignoring the outrage of the passers-by.

"Who is he?" whispered Annabel.

Without averting his gaze, Bert swallowed hard and managed a quivering reply. "It's Josh."

As he approached, his plight became clear. Tough-looking, with a granite-hard chin and flattened nose, Josh was nevertheless painfully thin, his clothes hanging from his hungry frame like heavy blankets thrown over a clothes line. His eyes were dark-ringed from lack of sleep and his hands and feet, which were bare, were streaked with dirt. Although he appeared in a desperate state, something about him spoke of callousness and brooding anger.

"Hello, *Burrt*," he said, stepping right up to the young couple, using Rooster's stretched pronunciation of his name, "where have you been then, my dear old friend?" The last few words, laced with sarcasm, were forced through gritted teeth and Bert took a slight step backwards, catching the threat in the little lad's voice. Annabel gripped his arm tighter still, reassuring him. Josh gave her a fleeting glance, then sneered accusingly, "I've been looking for you, ever since you decided to turn your back on me."

An icy, dangerous silence settled between them. Despite the throbbing noise all around, it was as if they were cocooned in their own separate world, where no one was aware of their existence; no one, that is, except for this ragged, sinister little boy standing unblinking, waiting.

With a trembling hand, Bert wiped a smear of sweat from his brow. The desire to run, break free, put all of this behind him, was overwhelming. But then, as if she realised, Annabel tightened her grip still further. He shot her a glance, then turned once more to Josh. "I couldn't get in," he blurted out, lying without thinking. "She wouldn't let me past the door, cagey old mare."

Nodding slowly, Josh's narrowed eyes roamed over Bert and settled on the canvas bag looped over his shoulder. "Strange that, because when I went round to see what had happened to you, the Peelers were all over the place like lice. They nabbed me, Bert old friend, took me down the clink and told me all about it, you see, every single little detail. You'd been there, got up the chimney, just as we'd planned. But when I wouldn't say a dicky, they put me up before the beak, me old friend. My good friend Bert, you..." His voice trailed off, the last word hanging in the air, like a blow ready to fall. The seconds crawled by, until at last his voice contorted into a mask of red, virulent hatred and he screeched, "*LIAR!*"

Like a caged animal unexpectedly set free, Josh sprang forward, his hands closing round Bert's throat and they crashed to the ground, feet and fists flailing in wild desperation. Josh was in a frenzy, his eyes wild with malignant anger, his arms like coiled steel, strong and powerful. In a tangled mess of legs and arms, Josh gradually got the better of his adversary. Bert, his lungs bursting with the exertion of trying to keep his attacker at bay, wriggled and struggled beneath his wild, merciless friend, but it was no good.

The first fist cracked against his jaw, sending his senses buzzing inside his head. Blindly, he parried a second, but a third struck him hard against the ear and he squealed, trying to turn away from a fourth, knowing defeat was close. Somewhere beyond Josh's shoulder, he saw Annabel... saw her grab Josh by the hair and yank him backwards with surprising strength. It was all the chance Bert needed. His right fist landed with a solid crack against Josh's chin and the little urchin fell back, dazed and hurt.

"Come on," cried Annabel, pulling Bert to his feet as a crowd of curious, baying onlookers pressed in around them, "let's get out of here!"

All at once, Bert found himself being pulled along, dazed and hurt. His jaw throbbed where Josh's blows had landed so heavily against his face. Turning to look behind him, he saw the semi-conscious Josh propping himself up on one elbow, blood dripping from his mouth and nose. One concerned stranger stooped to help, but Josh swatted away their proffered hand and got uncertainly to his feet. He ignored those around him who, very quickly, realised that here was a boy who did not need, perhaps even resented, help, so they melted away and left Josh to climb to his feet and glare at his erstwhile friend. Spitting out a curse, he turned and disappeared into the confusion of the day.

Trusting Annabel implicitly, Bert allowed himself to be dragged further away. She'd helped him in the fight, something which might have brought him shame once, but now caused his heart to swell with gratitude. Josh was a wiry and experienced street fighter. If it hadn't been for Annabel's intervention, things might well have turned out very differently. It could all so easily be Bert lying dazed and defeated on the cold cobbles.

So, as they moved ever deeper into the throng of everyday people going about their daily lives, a huge grin spread across his face. His heart pounded, not due to their running so fast to reach the first pawnbroker's shop, but to the warm glow spreading through him. And, with her hand in his, so warm and reassuring, he did not think he had ever felt happier.

* * *

Branching out from the main street, a labyrinth of narrow, winding lanes led them to where pawnbrokers plied their trade.

Coming to the first entrance, the profession's sign of three large balls hanging high above, they paused and exchanged uncertain looks. Squeezing his hand, Annabel pushed open the door, setting the bell clattering, announcing their arrival.

Dim and sweaty, the shop brimmed with a mass of upturned junk, crammed to the rafters with personal effects and larger items, such as chairs, stools and tables. Cabinets and shelves groaned with an abundance of ornaments and clocks of every shape and size. Lost in the wonders all around, Bert eyed the array of items, some cheap, some valuable, which cluttered his vision. Each bore a ticket, upon which was scrawled a number, written in a spidery hand. Many were encrusted with a thick layer of dust, betraying how long they had sat on their shelves, forgotten and neglected. The many poor of the area would come to this place, giving up precious possessions (either their own, or stolen ones – it was all the same to the pawnbrokers) as security against a loan. Not many returned to repay and claim back their security, despite the money offered being such a paltry sum to begin with.

Wide-eyed, Bert knew this time would not be any different. Why should it be, even though he felt sure that the jewels he carried in his pockets and canvas bag were worth a small fortune?

In the corner, lost amongst the heaving expanse of items, was the vague shadow of man seated behind a wire mesh hatch. Bert took a step closer.

The pawnbroker sat huddled over a pocket watch, tenderly tinkering at its mechanism with a minute screwdriver. He hardly stirred as the bell sounded on his door and now, deep in concentration, his dark, hooded eyes did not raise.

Hesitating, Bert gave Annabel a questioning look. She shrugged and tentatively knocked on the mesh.

With the merest tensing of his thin shoulders, the pawnbroker paused in his endeavours and waited. With a slight dig in his side, Annabel urged Bert to move. He dipped into his bag and brought out the first piece of jewellery, a large, purple-stoned brooch, which he pushed through the narrow opening in the bottom of the mesh. The pawnbroker eyed it with little interest, feeling it between forefinger and thumb. Bert noticed how long and white those fingers were, like worms oozing over the surface of the gemstone, gauging its value. Tapping the gold with a single blackened nail, he muttered something to himself before abruptly pushing the brooch back through the grill. "A shilling," he spat, after a long pause.

"You can't be serious," snapped Annabel, but Bert squeezed her arm, his other hand coming up, palm outwards in warning. For a moment, anger flared in her eyes, but then she caught his wink and she understood. Bert produced a heavy gold necklace which he carefully set down beside the brooch.

The pawnbroker relied on good acting skills to keep his emotions well hidden, and Bert knew this. Even so, confronted by the sheer weight and quality of the precious metal laid out before him, the pawnbroker forgot himself and let out a long, low whistle.

A heavy silence hung in the air as the pawnbroker lifted the necklace and studied it with the same care he'd shown with the brooch. Composure recovered slightly, the pawnbroker clicked his tongue, shook his head, and pushed the necklace back towards the young couple. "I couldn't give you more than a florin for that."

Bert swept up both pieces and spoke with barely contained fury, his impatience thick in his voice. "You must think we're stupid," he said and turned to go.

"I know *what* you are," breathed the man menacingly.

Pulling up sharp, Bert wondered if there might be some recognition between them. He couldn't be sure, but then he looked into the man's face for the first time. Beyond the grill, a hideous, ghoulish face stared back at him, thin grey skin stretched over a prominent nose and jaw, the eyes sunken and black. Like death.

Bert shuddered and pulled Annabel away by the arm, slamming the door behind them, the bell clanging once more through the shop.

"Oh my God, Bert. He was horrible. I didn't like him, not one bit," said Annabel. She stopped and gave Bert a hard stare. "Does he know you?"

Trying to sound brave, Bert forced a short chuckle. "Nah. He just thinks he does." Inside, his stomach turned to water. To give himself something to do and avoid her eyes, he rummaged through the bag. "It's just his way of trying to dupe us – throw us off-guard, offering us less than their real value, that's all."

"Perhaps he was being truthful – perhaps they're not really worth anything."

"Annabel, he knows *exactly* what this stuff is worth. You saw him when he picked up the necklace. He couldn't find the words for a moment or two. No," Bert shook his head, "he knows they're worth a pretty penny or two, mark my words. What we've got to do is find somebody who's at least willing to give us half of their true value. And that, dearest Annabel, is a lot more than a florin, so come on, we have a lot of work still to do."

* * *

They spent the best part of the next two hours scouring the streets, searching out various pawnbrokers and moneylenders, but having little success. The closest they got to nearly giving up their treasure was when one little man offered a guinea. A guinea, considered Bert, was more than he'd ever owned in his life, but even that was nowhere near the items' true worth. So they pressed on but, as each door closed behind them, their gloom deepened. Nobody was going to part with anything substantial, that much was painfully clear.

Eventually, depressed and miserable, they wandered into the park. Sitting by the lake, they threw blades of grass into the water and watched their dreams go drifting by.

"What are we going to do?" asked Annabel softly, all her previous bravado long since gone, replaced by sullen defeat. "All that hope," she continued, her voice so tiny, like the little girl she was, "ripped away in a single morning." Resting her head against Bert's shoulder, she sniffed, trying to hold back her tears.

Bert didn't move. He didn't want to. He knew her words were truthful. What a fool he'd been, to think that he, a creature of the streets, could ever hope to make something of his life. Despite the chance of riches the jewels and coins offered, they were as worthless as autumn leaves if he couldn't sell them. Gingerly, he slipped his arm around her, drawing her close. The only good thing that had come out of any of this was Annabel, so he shouldn't be too downhearted. He'd never known wealth, but perhaps now he'd found something worth far more. He kissed the top of her head and, when she didn't resist, he drew her that little bit closer. They sat together in silence, watching the lake and a family of ducks drifting by. Fatigue slowly took hold and their eyes grew heavy until eventually, and irresistibly, they began to close.

Chapter Ten

The Square in Time

It wasn't usual for Jamie to accept his mum's invitation to join her in a bit of window-shopping, but when she mentioned her itinerary included Hamilton Square, he couldn't resist. An overwhelming urge to explore that area gripped him, and had done ever since he'd returned from the house. Since then, as his dreams grew increasingly vivid, he'd conjured images of dark backstreets, grim shop fronts, sinister figures lurking in the shadows. He didn't know what he would discover when he got there, but he couldn't ignore the chance to find out. Sitting on the edge of his bed, he stared at his hands, ticking off the strange, interweaving scenes which populated his night. He believed they might be something more than mere dreams – messages perhaps from the past … or warnings.

His mum called him and he quickly grabbed his shoes. There was no point trying to find an explanation for what was happening; it was beyond explanation. Ever since he'd fallen asleep in that house, his sleeping hours had been filled with the most realistic dreams he had ever experienced. The places, smells, sounds and characters were so natural, they could not have been the product of his imagination, however fertile that might be. Were they memories from books he'd read, or films he's seen… or were they actual events? Had he somehow 'slipped' into another time, another dimension? Could such things even be possible?

There was another shout from below and he stood up. "Coming!" he called back. Wherever the answers lay, perhaps Hamilton Square was as good a place as any to start searching for them.

They boarded the number 10 bus from the top of the street and settled down for the journey. Jamie, always uncomfortable at sharing any sort of outing with his mum, stared out of the window and hoped nobody he knew had spotted him. If they had, he'd be called 'sissy' or 'a weed' for allowing himself to be pulled along by his mum. No one else from school did such a thing, for no one *allowed* themselves to be so humiliated.

The policeman, on duty atop a raised platform in the centre of Duke Street, waved the bus through and they clattered across the bridge and headed towards town. Narrowing his eyes, Jamie focused in on the policeman. He'd never noticed him on any of his trips to Birkenhead before now. Curious, he said, without turning, "Mum, what is that policeman doing?"

He glanced across at his mum, who appeared deep in concentration as she checked the contents of her purse. She didn't look up. Perhaps he should tell her his troubles, confide in her his mounting fears. The latest dream had been dark and thick with the threat of… *something*. Two children, creeping through narrow streets, trying to find a buyer for their wares, encountering a man whose presence reeked of evil intentions. The pawnbroker, a terrifying man with features cast from cold, hard granite, and eyes that burned with a livid intensity, filled with hatred… but hatred of what? What possible danger could those children hold for him? Or had Jamie mistaken the man's emotion? Dreams did that, contorting meaning, disguising the truth. Could jealousy, envy or greed have made the man seem so wicked, so dangerous? Certainly, he appeared to be someone capable of anything. Intimidation, violence, even murder.

Jamie shuddered at the memory of that ghoulish face. Could such a character ever have existed? If he did, then his shop might still be near to the Square. Possibly.

He turned again to take another look at the policeman.

Blinking, Jamie rubbed his eyes and stared again. An icy coldness ran across his shoulders.

The policeman was not there.

"Are you all right?"

Jamie, startled by his mum's question, snapped his head up. Was his imagination now playing tricks with him outside of his dreams, he wondered? He forced a smile. "Of course. Just thinking."

Frowning slightly, his mum said, without humour, "Yes, well, that's something you haven't been doing much of lately."

"*Mum.*" Turning away, he looked out through the grimy window again and gazed at the many shoppers streaming along the pavements. A scene not so unlike the one which had confronted Bert on his visit.

Bert.

Where had that name come from, he wondered, biting his lip. Was it the boy's, the one in his dreams?

Suddenly they arrived. The jerk of the vehicle coming to a halt cut off his meandering thoughts. Passengers began to stream off the bus. Impatiently, his mother pulled him to his feet. Stepping down into the throng, Jamie again compared this modern, chaotic world to the one experienced by Bert. Traffic trundled by, but of a different type to that of a hundred or more years ago. There were no longer any horse-drawn carriages and trolley buses to dodge and dip between. In their place were taxis, cars and buses, revving engines and belching exhaust fumes. He doubted Bert would recognise anything around him now, so much had changed. Perhaps the same would be true for the pawnbroker's shop. Would there be anything left, or would the bulldozers already have cleared it to make room for yet another housing estate? Perhaps there wouldn't be anything worth finding.

His mum had a hairdresser's appointment and when she stopped outside the shop and asked him if he'd like to come inside, the horror he felt must have shown on his face. She laughed. "Jamie, you'd think I'd asked you to carry out a bank robbery." Shaking her head, she delved into her purse and dropped a few coins into his hand. "Don't go too far."

Jamie nodded towards the underground railway station on the opposite side of the street. "I'll just be over there." A dark look came over her face, so he gave her a reassuring smile, "Mum, I'll be right there. No one's going to take me away."

She wasn't convinced. "You've got your mobile?" Reaching into his pocket, he produced the phone. "Good. Call me if there is any problem, you understand? Anything at all."

"I will, Mum. See you in an hour, yeah?"

She took him by the arms, pulled him to her and planted a huge kiss on his cheek, filling him with embarrassment. She stroked his hair, her eyes roaming over his face. "I'm worried about you. Ever since that night you…" Her voice trailed away and she sighed. "All right. An hour."

He walked off towards the station, aware of his mum's eyes boring into his back, but determined not to look round. Resolutely, he strode on, not sure what he was going to do or where he was going to go. All he knew was that he had to find a clue; anything that would lead him to the past.

* * *

The librarian behind the desk was efficient and helpful. She showed him to the shelves in which were stored the red-bound *Kelly's Directories* and he immediately ran his finger along each spine, trying to find inspiration from any of the dates embossed there. None sprang out at him. The clues in his dreams pointed at the late Victorian or early Edwardian periods. Workhouses, Peelers, cobbled streets. In fairness, he was looking at a stretch of almost eighty years or more. Huffing in frustration, he randomly pulled a volume from the shelf and took it to one of the large tables arranged in the centre of the reference library floor. Carefully, he leafed through the pages.

Sometime later, he grew aware of a presence at his shoulder and turned to see the librarian smiling down at him. "What is it you're looking for, exactly?"

Hesitantly at first, he slowly began to tell her about pawnbrokers and Hamilton Square and how he was trying to find out where their shops might have been. "I'm pretty much in the dark about dates, but I'm sure it was at a time before cars."

"Nineteenth century then. Or thereabouts."

"I think so."

"Is this for a school project or something?"

"Yes," he lied instantly, grateful that she'd unwittingly offered him the perfect reason for his search. "Yes, that's exactly what it is. We're supposed to research a crime, or crimes, that took place round about here in those days. Something to do with a pawnbroker."

She listened studiously, then crossed over the room to a large cabinet and pulled out some drawers. He followed her and saw she cradled several large rolls in her arms. Bringing them with her, she laid them out on Jamie's table. "These are old street maps," she explained. "They show the street layout of this area from well over a hundred years ago. We can cross-reference the names of streets with details from *Kelly's*. And, of course," she continued, seeming to feed off Jamie's enthusiasm, "there are newspapers. We have archives going back nearly one hundred and eighty years. If there was a crime committed, then it will almost certainly have been reported. Have you any clues about dates?"

Jamie shrugged and gave a disappointed shake of his head.

"Nothing at all? No hints, however vague?"

He thought for a moment. A memory stirred. "There was a mention..." He screwed up his eyes and tried desperately to remember. "Birkenhead Union Workhouse," he said at last.

"Ah!" she cried in triumph, "Then we have it. Birkenhead Union Workhouse was opened in the early eighteen-sixties, so..."

Like conspirators in a dastardly deed, they began to search in earnest.

When Jamie's mobile went off, the librarian gave him a frosty glare, coupled with some sharp words: "You shouldn't have that switched on, you know, not in here." She pointed to the signs pinned in various locations around the room. As if to give weight to her words, an old man in the far corner looked up from his newspaper and gave Jamie an accusing stare.

Jamie took the reproach, muttered an apology and wandered into the corridor, snapping open his phone to reveal that the caller was his mum. Groaning, he slowly pressed the mobile to his ear. "Yes, Mum?" He prepared himself for the onslaught he was about to receive. He was half an hour late and nowhere near the underground. If he was in trouble before, he was close to certain death now.

Returning to the reference library after a fearful ear-bashing, he found the librarian holding up several photocopied sheets. "I've got something very interesting for you, young man."

* * *

They journeyed home in silence, Jamie keeping his face pressed against the glass of the bus and away from the mask of fury his mother wore. She'd picked him up outside the library and marched him back to the nearest bus stop, berating him about his unacceptable and thoughtless behaviour. Did he do these things deliberately? Was he trying to put her in a mental home? He suffered the bombardment in silence and now, as he sat like a rock next to her, despite everything he gave himself a tiny little cheer of congratulation. With the help of the librarian, he'd discovered something which made his puzzling dreams meaningful. The next time he ventured into Hamilton Square, he knew exactly where he'd be going.

Chapter Eleven

Saved in the Park

He didn't know how long they had slept for. Blinking open his eyes to find the sunlight still strong but the day much later, he sat up and stretched. Very few people were in the park now, which told him it was early evening. It was time they were moving on, find somewhere to spend the night, seek out some food perhaps. Shaking himself like a dog, Bert reached out to touch Annabel, rouse her from sleep… and froze.

A cry caught in his throat. For one, wild moment he had an uncontrollable urge to run, to flee as fast as his legs would carry him. But nothing would move. Muscles had fused together, fear gripping him in a steel-like vice. Beside him, Annabel continued sleeping. She may as well be a thousand miles away for there was nothing he could do, or say, to warn her of the danger they now faced.

He stood there, with his back against the setting sun, a brooding, enormous and silent shape, the wide brim of his hat casting his face in deep shadow. But there was no mistaking who he was. The pawnbroker, the first one they had visited.

The mouth split into a sneering grin, teeth impossibly white against the black face. The grin of one tasting victory. Bert had no words to describe this vision of wickedness. Annabel would know, but Annabel slept on soundlessly, undisturbed, in blissful ignorance. Then the pawnbroker moved.

* * *

Bert's scream caused Annabel to waken with a jolt. Rolling over, her eyes doing cartwheels as she struggled to overcome her disorientation, she could hear the unmistakeable sounds of a scuffle. Heart pounding, she leaped up, half-expecting to see Josh swinging punches, battering poor Bert to the ground. What she actually did see chilled her to the core. Bert and the pawnbroker, wrestling with one another on the grassy bank, Bert, a fury of arms and legs, desperately lashing out at the much more powerful figure attacking him. Without a sound, and with a dismissive, arrogant ease, the pawnbroker swatted away each of Bert's feeble blows, pinned back his arms and slapped him hard across the face. Reeling backwards, he fell to the ground, snail trails of blood running from his nostrils.

The blow stunned Annabel into action. Screaming at the top of her voice, she launched herself at the man like a wildcat, hands clawing at his face and neck, nails raking through flesh. He tried in vain to deflect her, but she was too quick, and they tumbled to the grass in a confused heap. As they hit the hard earth, his powerful frame landed on top of her. The force of the impact knocked the breath out her and Annabel lay still, stunned. It was all the time the pawnbroker needed. Sensing victory, he heaved himself to his feet, and, through a swirling mist of flashing lights and weird, dancing shapes, she saw him in the process of aiming a vicious kick. Recovering quickly, she rolled away. His foot hit thin air. Unbalanced, and with all his attention on the girl, he did not notice Bert climbing to his feet, shaking off the blow to his face. Bert attacked, diving full stretch at the man's legs, and bowled him over.

Bert was not going to let the advantage slip. His small fists pummelled at the pawnbroker's face, the blows causing blood to spew out from his lip and nose.

Not relenting, Bert called for Annabel to help. The pawnbroker, arms protecting his face, would soon recover from this initial shock. They had to beat him hard, smash him into the ground if necessary and make good their escape.

"Annabel, Annabel, come on. Put your boot into this monster's head!" he called.

But Annabel didn't respond. Angry and desperate, Bert took a chance and shot her a quick glance. The scene before him gripped him with a renewed fury.

There was Josh, that snivelling, evil, twisted traitor, grappling with Annabel, forcing her down, overpowering her and preventing her from helping. Bert let out a roar and Josh stopped. He looked up, eyes wide with fright, and stumbled to his feet. Stepping away from Annabel who was crying uncontrollably beneath him, he raised both hands. "Now then, Bert old lad, don't you be doing anything hasty." And then, incredibly, he smiled.

Bert's anger blinded him to the other, perhaps more dangerous threat of the pawnbroker. Determined to smash Josh to pieces, Bert, fists already bunching for the assault, stood up, took a step forward, and immediately received a crushing blow in the back of his head, which slammed him face down into the ground.

He lay there, mouth full of soil, and tried to find the strength to get up. Confused, pain lancing through his neck, his senses reeled but he managed to roll over, the world swirling before his eyes. Spitting out blood and earth, he put a hand behind him to steady himself. He would get up and fight it out, but his will alone was not enough. It was all too much and he had overestimated his own strength. No longer able to hold his weight, his arm gave way and he fell back, grunting with the pain. Josh filled his sight, his face a mask of triumph, his teeth flashing as he cocked back his own fist, ready to smash it into Bert's face.

"Wait!"

The pawnbroker's voice sounded shrill. It was the first time he had spoken since the attack had begun. "Wait," he said again, pulling back Josh's arm. He bent down, gripping Bert's face in his own grimy hand. They stared into each other's eyes. Feverishly, the man rummaged through Bert's pockets, pulling out a handful of the jewellery. His mouth opened, stinking breath steaming into Bert's nostrils. "Where are the other gems?" he snarled. His fingers tightened and Bert winced. "I want all of them, you miserable wretch."

"Here they are, guv," said Josh, stepping into Bert's line of sight, holding up the canvas bag in triumph.

Snatching it from Josh's grasp, the pawnbroker rooted around inside the bag. He brought out a bundle of bracelets and let the ropes of gold slide through his fingers. "This is a pretty lot you have here, but I want to know where you got it from. There's more, I know it – now, tell me where you got these gems, you little rat!"

"You said they were worthless," Bert managed, his defiance not leaving him for a moment, despite the fear building up inside.

"I lied," spat the pawnbroker simply. "Now, I'll ask you again, and if I get no answer," he gestured with a jerk of his head to Josh, "the girl gets to lose her pretty face."

Twisting his head, Bert gasped as Josh jerked Annabel's head back by the hair, his other hand producing a blade that glinted evilly in the evening sunlight. He saw her struggling uselessly in Josh's strong grip. "Don't tell them, Bert. Don't tell them anything."

Bert felt his stomach turn to water. It was no use, there was nothing he could do. His shoulders slumped, capitulation washing over him like a torrent. He would have to tell them.

"All right," he began desperately, his voice losing all of his former defiance, "I'll tell you where I found them. Please let her go."

The pawnbroker grinned. "Tell first, then she goes free."

"How do I know you'll keep your word?"

The pawnbroker paused for effect. "You don't."

With his world in turmoil, he knew he had little or no choice but to tell the pawnbroker what he wanted to know. Perhaps there was some shred of decency about him and once the jewels were in his possession, perhaps he'd let them both go free. Bert swallowed hard.

"The house," he began slowly, knowing lies were not an option as Josh already knew most of the original plan devised by old Rooster. "Rooster found it, see. A big house outside of town. He told Josh and me to go and take a look. But Josh didn't turn up," he threw an accusing glance at his old friend, "so I was all alone. The old woman, she let me in and –"

"Just like that?"

"No, I tricked her. She thought I was a sweep." Another glance towards Josh, who knew that the story so far was true. Only now, with Annabel quiet and still in Josh's arms, did Bert deviate from the truth. "So she left me to do my work and in the big dining room, under a statue, I saw that there was a drawer."

"A drawer? What sort of drawer?"

Bert's imagination was working overtime, but he knew the introduction of the statue was a gamble. Somehow, he had to keep the truth from these villains. Any hesitation on his part would reveal that he was fabricating the whole story. "A hidden compartment… but it hadn't been shut properly. So I went over to have a look, and there they were. The jewels."

"Lucky find, eh?"

"Rooster had said there would be something there. He said he had heard of a legend, a story, that the old woman was one of the richest old dears in the whole country and that her fortune was hidden somewhere in that house."

"That's right, guv," came Josh's voice. "That's what old Cockbird told us all right."

The pawnbroker eyed Josh suspiciously. Then he turned back to Bert, gripping his face harder still. "If you're lying to me…"

"It's the truth," Bert lied, but managing to keep his eyes firmly locked on the pawnbroker's. "I took what I could and ran like a whippet until I was far away from the house. Only thing was, when I got to town, some people saw me. They chased me, calling me a thief, which I am of course, but I took off faster than ever and hid in some old, falling-down houses. That's where I met Annabel. We thought about what we should do and decided to try our luck in getting some money for what I'd taken. That's why we came to you. And that's it – the truth, I swear it."

The pawnbroker looked at him for a long time, considering Bert's words carefully. Bert knew his story sounded plausible enough, if just a little coincidental, but he felt sure the pawnbroker had fallen for it. If he still had doubts, he might well decide to investigate for himself, possibly sending Josh to the house for a poke around.

With a sudden jerk, the pawnbroker let go of Bert's face and stood up, dusting the dirt from his trousers with his hat.

"What do I do with her?" asked Josh, still gripping Annabel by her hair. She hadn't moved throughout Bert's fiction and now, looking into those huge, round eyes, his heart swelled.

The pawnbroker sniggered, a horrible, cackling sound. "Stripe her," he said, voice full of relish.

Yelping in fear and anger, Bert scrambled to his feet, desperate to race to Annabel's aid, but the pawnbroker grabbed him around the waist and lifted him into mid-air. Kicking and crying, Bert watched helplessly as Josh slowly drew back his arm, preparing the thin knife blade to slice through Annabel's flesh. "NO!" he roared at the top of his voice, his legs flailing as he squirmed and wriggled to break free of the pawnbroker's grip. But it was useless, the man's strength was too great and he realised, in that single, dreadful moment, that there was nothing he could do to prevent the inevitable. Throwing back his head, he let out a single, piercing scream of total despair.

But the help, arriving as it did, came from an unlooked-for source.

Approaching the group in stealthy silence, a tall man seemingly emerged out of thin air, gripping a silver-topped walking stick in both hands, which he used like a sort of spear to ram the point hard into the pawnbroker's solar-plexus. Squealing, the pawnbroker folded from the waist, dropping Bert to the ground. When he looked up, he saw the stranger's arm coming around in a long arc. The walking stick landed with an awful crack across Josh's knife-wielding arm. Clutching at his wrist, Josh screamed and staggered back. The knife fell and Annabel was free.

With the pawnbroker writhing in agony on the ground, Bert raced across to where Annabel sat, weeping openly, held securely in the stranger's arms. Bert looked at the man properly for the first time and saw how elegant the stranger appeared, dressed in a dark, long-tailed jacket, grey, pin-striped trousers and top hat, the mark of a true gentleman – perhaps even a government official of some sort. Whoever or whatever he might be, Bert felt such gratitude that he forgot all propriety and plunged his face into the man's arms, his tears coming in an unchecked torrent.

A sound caused them all to come to their senses. It was the pawnbroker, his voice cracking in a mixture of pain and fury as he got to his feet clutching his stomach, his other hand holding a knife of his own. "You'll pay for this, you interfering swine!"

In a blur, the stranger rose, again using the walking stick with expert precision to knock the pawnbroker's knife-arm back and up. In a single, flowing movement, he stepped in close, right foot leading, and delivered an uppercut directly under the pawnbroker's chin with the boss-end of the stick, snapping his head back. As the pawnbroker teetered, the stranger rapped him across the temple, sending him crumpling to the ground like a burst balloon. He lay unconscious, his breath rattling in his chest.

"Oh dear, lummy, oh blimey," said Josh, who had been temporarily forgotten in all the mayhem. Clutching his arm, he hobbled away into the distance, leaving his own knife lying deserted in the grass.

Releasing a long sigh, the stranger turned to Bert and smiled. "I'm not sure what all of this was about, young man, but I've a suspicion it wasn't anything good."

Snuggling up next to Annabel, Bert nodded frantically. "Nothing good at all, sir. Thank you so very much, sir. Without you, I don't think we would have got out of this alive. No, indeed not, sir, indeed not."

"I think you had better come along with me and explain it all, young man. Don't you agree?"

Nodding limply, Bert helped Annabel to her feet. "I do, sir." He glanced over to where the pawnbroker lay spread-eagled on the ground. Without a word, Bert bent down and gathered together the jewels lying amongst the grass. He caught the stranger watching. He cleared his throat. "I can explain everything, sir. I truly can."

Grunting, the stranger took hold of Annabel's hand and strode away. After a few moments, and one more glance towards the pawnbroker, Bert followed.

* * *

They sat around a massive oak table, polishing off bowls of delicious soup with hunks of fresh bread. Both had bathed, had their cuts and bruises tended and now they were clean and warm, dressed in new clothes, their own rags having been cast into the fire by a large, kind house-maid, who now took their finished bowls away with a friendly smile.

At the far end, their rescuer, who had introduced himself as Mr John Taylor, sipped a cup of hot tea and smiled. Replacing the teacup in its saucer with intricate care, he studied the two children for a moment and asked softly, "Do you feel ready to talk?"

Bert had waited for this moment ever since Mr Taylor had saved him and Annabel, wondering what to say, how to convince this true gentleman that he was not a bad person. He knew he'd done wrong, but it was circumstance, not his wayward nature, which had made him a thief. He wrestled with his choice of words, just as before when the pawnbroker had confronted him. Then, he had lied, to save his own skin. This time, however, there was no threat, just the open, honest face of the man who had saved his life, and almost certainly had saved Annabel from the most dreadful attack imaginable. Too many lies had governed Bert's life up until this moment and now it was time to wipe the slate clean and begin afresh. Josh and his like were in another universe and Bert wanted nothing more to do with any of it. Josh, totally under the pawnbroker's power, had thrown in his lot with that maniac. What they threatened to do to Annabel was too much; it simply wasn't right.

Bert drew a deep breath, his face never leaving Mr Taylor's as he told the entire story from beginning to end, leaving nothing out, every word truthful, no matter how difficult it might be.

His tale finished, Bert slumped back in his chair, breathless but relieved to have unburdened himself. Annabel's hand found his, giving it a little squeeze. Her eyes were filled with admiration and, Bert hoped, something else.

Leaning forward, Taylor rested his chin on his upturned hands. "A remarkable story, Bert."

"It's true, sir. Every word."

"I don't doubt it."

Bert shot a glance across to Annabel, whose lovely face regarded him with openness and quiet encouragement. "Will you give me up to the Peelers now, sir? I wouldn't blame you if you did, but sir, Annabel, she never had anything to do with any of it. She's innocent, sir, I swear it and I don't –"

"I'm not going to *give you up* to anyone, Bert. Neither you nor Annabel. What I do wish to do is learn as much as I can about the people you have shared your short and eventful life with. This Rooster person, for example. He sounds quite a character."

"He's more than that, sir," said Bert. "He's a monster. He controls a gang of boys, sending them out to do all sorts of dishonest business, but never getting his own hands dirty. Very clever, and very dangerous."

"I'm sure. And I'm also sure that you needn't bother with him, or any of his like, ever again. What do you think, Annabel?"

Annabel stared into Mr Taylor's strong, honest face and nodded, her jawline reddening slightly. "I think I would very much like to stay here, sir," she said. "I feel safer here than I can ever remember feeling about anywhere." She shifted uneasily in her chair, clearing her throat before continuing, "If I could make so bold, sir..."

He frowned slightly. "Yes, go on."

"We'd like to repay you for your kindness, sir – in service, of course, sir," she added hastily. She gripped Bert's hand harder still. "And Bert would make an excellent footman, in time."

Bert snorted dismissively, regretting it almost immediately when he saw her horrified look. He knew what she said was for the best. Straightening his back, he gave his best attempt at being military and correct. "It would be an honour, sir."

Taylor shook his head. "You're both far too young for that." He took a breath, appearing to weigh up any number of solutions in his mind. Annabel and Bert waited, holding one another's hands. Bert felt convinced life was about to deal him another cruel blow. If Mr Taylor could not offer them a chance to start again, there really was no other course to save themselves from the likes of Rooster and the pawnbroker but the obvious one – they would have to return to the workhouse.

Taylor coughed, as if to catch their attention. When he spoke again, his smile seemed a little tremulous, hinting at a slight embarrassment but for what, Bert could not fathom. "I think, all things considered, it would be best for you stay here, but not in the capacity you have suggested. My own children are grown now. George has begun a commission in my old regiment back in India, and Clarissa has left for York with her new husband. So, I am alone, you see." He paused and looked at them, once more appearing a little unsure of himself. "What I am trying to say is that you can stay here as my own adopted children. For as long as you wish. I have discussed it with my wife."

"Your wife, sir?"

Nodding, Taylor held Bert's stare. "She's not very well, I'm afraid. You will meet her, when the time is right."

"But sir," said Annabel breathlessly, "you really mean it? We can stay?"

"My wife and I have spoken, as I said, and she is of the opinion that no other solution could possibly be tenable. The decision, however, is up to you, naturally."

A new home, a new beginning… how could they refuse? Annabel, yelping with glee, bounced up and down on her seat, both fists crammed into her mouth. Bert, however, was always the wary one. He knew enough about the world to realize that nothing came without a price. He took a breath; there were questions he needed to ask. Leaning forward, his eyes never leaving their saviour's, he asked in a low, serious voice, "And the conditions, Mr Taylor?"

"What do you mean, Bert?"

"I mean, sir, giving no offence, are we to live here under any formal conditions… arrangements, rules, that sort of thing?"

"Oh Bert," snapped Annabel in despair, "how can you be so ungrateful?"

"No, he's quite right to ask," said Mr Taylor. He looked Bert squarely in the eyes. "There is one condition, Bert. Only one."

"I thought there might be."

"I want you to return the things you took from the house to their rightful owner."

Bert turned to Annabel. She held her breath. Slowly, Bert turned to look at Mr Taylor once more. There was a ghastly pause. Then Bert smiled. "I'd already decided to do that, anyway."

Annabel threw her arms around him and kissed him on the cheek. "Oh, Bert, you're an angel."

"Yes," said Bert, struggling to break free, "so stop trying to crush my flamin' wings!"

They were still laughing with the joy of it all as they settled down to sleep in their comfy new beds in their new home. All of their old fears buried, the thrill of a new life stretched out before them. For the first time since he couldn't remember when, Bert closed his eyes on a world without fear.

Chapter Twelve

Return to the House

Jamie stood and stared with great interest at his reflection in the bathroom mirror. From what he could tell, he appeared the same as usual – on the outside, at least. Those big, innocent eyes, the slightly up-turned nose, the lips some people said were too tight. An everyday sort of face, nothing special, nothing unique. Just as it had always looked. But it was beneath his features that Jamie experienced real change. He had grown older, more knowing and a good deal more serious. And all because of the dreams. They troubled him deeply, but the last one especially. This was not something conjured up by his subconscious, or a half-forgotten film he'd seen, or a book he'd read. This was *real*. Up until now, for the most part his memories of the de-tails had been sketchy, nothing more than broken, tangled-up images, voices and sounds, mixed together in a random jumble. But the dream from last night stayed with him, dominating his waking thoughts. He remembered everything in sharp, clear de-tail: people, their clothes, voices, even smells. The wind in the trees, the freshness of the grass, the warmth of the sun. Above all else, the most powerful image was that of the pawnbroker's face, so real Jamie could taste the foul breath steaming out of his cracked and twisted mouth.

He shivered and filled the wash basin with water, absently running a bar of soap through his fingers. Bizarrely, it was as if he'd been allowed a glimpse – no, more than that, a *physical insight* – into a whole episode from the past. It was as if his dreams had transported him back to a bygone age, one that had actually existed. It was an unbelievable idea, he knew that, but what if it was true? What if, in some absurd and impossible way, his dream world was a gateway into the past? And if it was, perhaps he could discover if the images he saw were true. Had it really happened? Surely not. Surely this was all down to his imagination…

He threw water over his face, reached for a towel and pressed it hard against his skin. Why him? Was it because of the house, that statue, the message? He barely remembered a chimney, and yet it was this that dominated his dreams. That and the treasure. The more he thought about it and tried to find an explanation, the more confused and frustrated he became. This was something way beyond his understanding.

Looking again at his reflection, he found nothing had grown any clearer. The same questions kept swirling around in his head, over and over, more so since his frustrating search around Hamilton Square and what he'd discovered at the library. The reports of crimes… of murder… Squeezing his eyes shut, he found the face of the pawnbroker coming towards him, mouth contorted into a snarl of rage.

His mother's voice broke into his thoughts. "Jamie? Telephone."

He snapped his eyes open, half-expecting the pawnbroker's face to be staring back at him from the mirror, but there was only his own reflection. He pulled the plug, turned and ran to the stairs, more eager to leave the image of the pawnbroker behind than he was to answer his mother's call.

"Who is it?" he asked breathlessly as he reached the bottom of the stairs. No one *ever* telephoned him.

His mum smiled. That infuriating 'know-it-all' sort of smile parents make when they think they know something they shouldn't. "It's Sarah," she said in a whisper and handed over the handset with a wink.

Jamie stopped and pulled a face, his stomach doing a somersault. Sarah Jarvis, phoning him? He took the receiver and waited for his mum to retreat. She did so reluctantly, stepping into the kitchen, closing the door quietly behind her. Jamie felt sure she was listening, but spoke into the phone nevertheless. "Hello?"

Sarah's voice came down the line, sounding sweet. "Hi, Jamie. It's me."

"Oh, hi," said Jamie, desperately trying to keep the awkwardness from his voice, not wanting to reveal how he felt. He hoped he sounded cool, but part of him suspected he was failing miserably as he asked breathlessly, "You are... er... you are still coming to tea, aren't you?"

"Of course," she said quickly. He thought she sounded slightly hurt. A long pause followed, during which Jamie felt sure she would hear his heartbeat pounding down the phone. Then, at last, that soft golden voice of hers once again: "Why, don't you want me to?"

"My God, yes," he gushed, "of course I do!" She giggled, the most wonderful giggle he'd ever heard. "I'm sorry, I didn't mean –"

"Don't be sorry, Jamie."

He almost groaned. The way she spoke his name... Swallowing hard, he continued, "It's just, well, I just, you know, thought that maybe you didn't really want to, maybe." He closed his eyes in intense embarrassment. God, what an idiot he was. His mouth had totally disconnected itself from his brain. If he wasn't careful, he might say something so utterly stupid she would be put off for life.

"Of course I still want to. I'm looking forward to it."

Unable to hide his relief, he blew out a long sigh. "Brilliant, thanks. Thanks, thanks a lot. I'm looking forward to it, too."

"That's good." She lowered her voice, sounding conspiratorial. "Listen, I've just had a call from Tim."

Jamie heart gave a little leap. "You did? When? Tell me what he said."

"He was talking about dreams and stuff."

"*Dreams*?" Jamie felt his shoulders tighten. His voice broke again as he took a breath and asked, not totally convinced he wanted to know the answer, "What kind of dreams?"

"He said he rang me because you two were banned from seeing each other, because of this business in the big house? Is that right?"

"Sort of." She obviously knew the whole story, so was this some test of his honesty? Or was she just playing silly games, the sort of games girls always play, especially very attractive and confident girls like Sarah Jarvis. She was so frustrating. At one turn nice and open, the other all secretive and stiff. But he liked her – liked her a lot. And Tim contacting her, well, that was good... wasn't it?

Desperate not to offend her and lose her friendship, he continued, trying not to sound as worried as he felt, "What did he say about the dreams?"

"That he'd been having strange dreams, that's all. He talked about a girl and a boy finding jewels and of them being chased by some weird bloke into a park and... well, just stuff."

Despite his best efforts, Jamie's voice cracked. "He said all that?" This was incredible news! The same dreams? Perhaps the same scenes! His grip on the receiver was wet, sweat breaking out on his face. He shook his head, not daring to believe the thoughts forming in his mind. It couldn't be possible – what he was hearing must be part of the same crazy, mad world into which he'd been transported. Hallucinations, all of it.

"Are you okay, Jamie?"

"What?" Her assured, mature voice broke his reverie. It should have made him feel calmer, but her revelation that Tim was experiencing similar phenomena brought him nothing but more anxiety, more self-doubt. If it was true, then it meant both of them had slipped into the same nightmarish world. He took a breath, gathering himself. "Yeah, I'm okay. Did he, er, say anything else?"

"Yes. He sounded frightened. He asked us to meet him at the big house today, at two o'clock."

"Oh God. I'm not sure... Sarah, what do I tell Mum?"

* * *

Jamie hated himself for lying to his mum, but what choice did he have? He tried to convince himself it was for the best; that sometimes a 'tiny' lie could eventually lead to a good outcome. So he told her he was meeting Sarah, which was true, to spend some time together in Central Park, which wasn't. He conveniently made no mention of Tim, knowing if he had, Mum would have gone up the wall. Convinced that Tim must be as frightened and confused as he was, Jamie simply had to see him, calm him down and reassure him that he wasn't going crazy.

So, he lied.

To maintain the pretence of going to the park, which was little more than a short stroll away, he had to leave his bike behind. Fearful his mum might follow him, after he waved his goodbyes he actually did go to the park and found a graffiti-covered bench upon which to wait and check. Once he felt certain that his mother had not left the house, he cut across the cricket pitch, skirted around the town centre and took an old woodland path that led to Bidston and what still remained of the original village.

As he plodded on through the trees, he found himself wondering if it was just his overactive imagination that was responsible for conjuring up so many images – especially those of the house, the jewels, the pawnbroker. However, when he reached the rise and looked out across a vista unchanged from his dreams, he realised none of this was of his making.

The house straddled the top of a rolling hill. Broad steps led down to vast grounds, the garden expertly laid out in a grid-like pattern. Despite approaching it from the same direction as before, the view struck him as much more real now. He'd spent a night in this place, lured to sleep by forces unseen and irresistible. His research at the library and the facts he'd uncovered convinced him that somehow, some way, he and Tim had both slipped through some form of gateway into an alternative existence, one accessed through dreaming.

With this theory ruminating in his mind, Jamie spotted Tim standing outside the main door with Sarah a step or two behind, gazing absently into the fountain. Something in Tim's demeanour struck him as not quite right. Even from this distance, he noticed the slumped shoulders, the pacing, the constant turning of his head from side to side as if he were expecting to see something – or someone. And not only Jamie. Someone unseen.

As he drew closer, Jamie saw it more clearly. Tim wasn't his usual tough self. He seemed sheepish, shy and on edge, his body shrunk into itself. His eyes, dark with shadow, darted around, confirming his anxiety, his fear of someone else coming upon them.

"You took your time!" snapped Tim as Jamie stepped up, ready to give a friendly grin, a fist-bump, perhaps. But Tim's annoyance took him by surprise and when Sarah joined them, all she could offer was a slight shrug of the shoulders.

This was not what Jamie had been expecting.

Without another word, Tim turned and tried the door, rattling the handle. It was locked. Tim looked at Jamie over his shoulder, showing no surprise. "It was like this before. Someone has been here since the police came, and shut the place up again. While

I was waiting for you, I had a good scout around and found another door, on the far side. It led to a cellar. Probably an old tradesman's entrance. Whoever looks after the house now either forgot about it, or didn't even realise it exists. Luckily for us, it's the perfect way to get in."

He shot a glance towards Sarah, who nodded and turned to Jamie. If Jamie had any misgivings, he didn't show them. The time for indecision had passed. "Let's go," he said and followed his friend to the rear, with Sarah some steps behind, to what Tim described as the tradesman's entrance.

A small flight of worn, weed-overgrown steps led to a green door, paint peeling from its warped timber frame. Putting his shoulder against it, Tim pushed it open, grunting with the exertion and stepped into the darkness beyond.

Despite the gloom, Jamie knew which direction to take. The dreams he and Tim shared were a better guide than any map.

"Wait," said Tim. He delved into his pocket and brought out his mobile and pressed the torch app. "Damn," he spat. "My phone's dead. But," he continued, rummaging through his pockets, "I had an idea this might happen, so I brought something, just in case." He produced a candle. Using a lighter, he put a flame to the wick and lit up the first few paces of the dank, forgotten cellar.

"There's a door straight ahead," said Jamie.

"You know that, too?" said Tim.

"I know everything."

Grunting, Tim led the way, candle held aloft. Trailing behind, Sarah found Jamie's hand and held it tight. They exchanged a look and they both smiled.

Soon, they were following a series of corridors that led to the dining room. Tim strode across to one of the tall, narrow windows on the far side and opened the heavy, white wood shutters. Daylight streamed in. Tim blew out the candle and they found themselves staring once again at the statue with its inscription.

But it was the chimney that grabbed their immediate attention, the finely-crafted surround appearing as pristine as if it had been made only yesterday. Below the gleaming mantle, the fireplace gaped huge, wide and black. Jamie gulped, knowing what had to be done.

* * *

Sarah waited, kicking her feet, blowing out her cheeks, clicking her tongue. Every so often she would stop and ask Jamie how long it had been, and every time Jamie told her to wait and not be so impatient. He sat on the floor with his back to the wall, trying to think of nothing, but all the time returning to the image of the pawnbroker. His big, ugly face peered at him through a mist of distant memories. Jamie hated it. It was a face he would have loved to extinguish, but no matter how hard he tried, he couldn't get it out of his mind.

When Tim finally reappeared, covered in dust and soot, he looked for all the world like an image of a boy chimney sweep that they had studied at school. All he needed was a flat cap to complete the picture. But there was something else, something about him, the way he stood, huge grin splitting his face, teeth gleaming white in the blackness of his dirt-streaked face, that made Jamie sit up. Gone was the uncertainty and fear from before, replaced by the Tim of old – confident and assured. Jamie held his breath and then Sarah gave whoop of glee. There, in Tim's fist, dangled a bundle of glittering, sparkling jewellery.

* * *

Later, after arranging with Tim to meet up the following day, Jamie took Sarah back home. They sat opposite each other at the dining room table, with Mum serving the tea. She'd made a big effort and Sarah, obviously impressed, ate everything set before her, smiling the whole time. Jamie, however, continued to worry. After he had produced the 'treasure', Tim announced he was staying behind to find more, but that they should go back to Jamie's to keep up the pretence. He'd see them tomorrow.

At first, Jamie had refused, but it was Sarah who had insisted, pointing out that if anything happened again, Jamie's mum would never forgive him. Now, poking his fork through his food, he knew Sarah was right, but nothing could shift the sense of dread brewing up inside him. He did his best to mask his growing worry, but failed.

"Not hungry?"

He looked up to see his mum standing there, eyes searching his features, knowing her son only too well, knowing he was hiding something.

"I wanted him to take me to the big old house," said Sarah quickly, before Jamie could offer his own explanation.

Snapping his head around, Jamie gaped at her. Mum drew in a breath. "Oh. You did?"

"Yes," she continued, her voice as calm and as confident as the one she used in class, "but he refused. He told me he couldn't, that he'd promised you he would not go there again."

Both mother and son stared in stunned silence.

"Jamie said *that*?" asked Mum at last, incredulously.

Popping a thin slice of ham into her mouth, Sarah nodded as she munched it down. "Yes. He told me how upset you were at what he'd done. So… I didn't push it."

His mum's eyes turned to Jamie, who merely pressed his lips together and shrugged. "My God," she muttered and went back to the kitchen in a sort of daze.

"What the hell are you –"

Sarah cut off his frantic whisper with an outstretched hand. "Just eat your tea, Jamie. Everything is going to be fine."

After peach melba ice-cream, they watched a film together, then Mum got out the Scrabble. Sarah won. Easily. Jamie, coming a miserable third, glowed with affection at this wonderful girl.

Later, they drank hot chocolate and munched cookies whilst Mum made herself scarce.

"I've had a great day," Sarah said, cupping both hands around her steaming cup.

"You mean that?"

"Of course I do – I wouldn't have said it otherwise. You're a really interesting guy, Jamie."

He squirmed. "I'm not."

"Yes, you are. You're so quiet in school, but today… What made you go to that house in the first place?"

"We came upon it by accident, but it was Tim who wanted to go inside. He's the brave one, not me."

"Yes, but you fell asleep there. Why didn't you leave, come back home?"

"That's the really crazy part. It was as if some force, a mysterious power, compelled me to find that room and go to sleep. Then came the dreams, of course. And they've never stopped."

She considered him for a long time over the brim of her mug.

"You don't believe me."

"It's not that," she said, placing the mug down on the low, glass-topped table in front of the sofa where they sat. "Weren't you afraid? I'd be terrified if I thought I'd have to stay there in that big old house all alone."

"I was, of course I was, but like I said, it was like some sort of invisible –"

"Power. Compelling you to stay. Yes, you said."

"And that's the part you can't understand."

"It's the part I find most fascinating, Jamie," she said and reached across to squeeze his hand. "That's what I mean when I say you're so interesting. Maybe you're some sort of psychic and you have extra-sensory perception or some such thing."

"I've never really considered it… I don't know, maybe you're right. But nothing like this has ever happened to me before."

"Maybe the house is a form of portal."

"Portal?"

"Yes, a worm-hole or whatever you want to call it. Brian Cox wrote about it. He said that –"

"Brian who?"

"Professor Brian – oh, never mind, it doesn't matter. But something has happened, Jamie. Something triggered those dreams."

"And those images of the pawnbroker."

They looked at one another for a long time without speaking.

When it was time for Sarah to go, Jamie took her to the door and waved her off as she strolled down the path towards her dad's car. She stopped and turned and his heart leaped up into his mouth as she came running back and kissed him on the cheek. Then she was gone and although in a way Jamie felt happier than he had for years, he also felt very empty and very alone.

"She's a lovely girl," said his mum softly, when he came back into the living room. She was tidying up the board game. Jamie watched her. He wanted it to be three hours ago, so that he could have this evening all over again. The house was so terribly quiet now. Without thinking, he asked, "When's Dad coming home?"

He saw his mum's back stiffen. She looked at him over her shoulder. There was no anger there, just resignation. She tried a brave smile. "You know the answer to that one."

Jamie nodded and sat down, fingering the television remote control, wishing he was just settling down to watch something with Sarah once more.

Mum came and sat down beside him. "What's up?" she asked.

Jamie shrugged. "I'm just missing him, that's all."

Putting her arms around him, Mum held him gently and lovingly as she whispered, "I know."

They sat like that for a long time.

* * *

When the police came it was as if the dreams were turning into nightmares. Tim was missing. He hadn't come home last night. Did Jamie know anything about it? Had he seen Tim? Had they been back to the old house?

Jamie lied again.

All evening, the guilt stayed with him.

That night, it took him a long, long time to fall asleep.

Chapter Thirteen

Rooster

In the oppressive gloom of his attic room, the only sound the constant drip of damp, the only companion the stench of rotting timbers, the man known as Rooster stooped at his table. This rotten, creaking, porous sponge that threatened to collapse at any moment, was his worktop. With a jeweller's glass fixed in his eye, he examined the mess of trinkets spread out before him. His hands were dextrous, expert at the craft, sorting out with surprising swiftness the almost worthless from the totally worthless. Every now and then he would lift a piece close to his face and scrutinise it with tender care, but almost always he would discard the piece, accompanying this with a muttered curse of despair.

He'd learned his trade from an early age on the streets. Abandoned by his widowed father, he'd worked his way through the ranks of the dispossessed, first as a guttersnipe living on his wits and his fists. London in the mid-1800s was no place for a homeless child, but somehow he had managed to scratch out a living. His dirt-encrusted fingernails and matted grey hair were a testament to a lifetime without soap and water. Born of the streets, he'd made his home in the filth and the squalor that oozed along the pavements; it was his kingdom and he knew no other way.

At around fifteen, he'd fallen in with a gang of thieves who had managed to find passage on an old steam-tramp ploughing its way from the Thames docks to Liverpool. From there, more by luck than design, the Peelers had made their presence felt and the gang broke up. Some had gone back to the dubious charms of the Empire's capital city; others had stayed in Liverpool. Rooster had hidden on board a ferry and crossed the River Mersey to Birkenhead.

It was nothing like London, if for no other reason but its size. The area close to the river where he made his base, continued to thrive. The great black ships that filled the great port of Liverpool disgorged their cargos twenty-four hours a day. The docks of Birkenhead were a breeding ground for corruption, vice and opportunity for thieves and scoundrels of every description. Along the promenade of Egremont, the millionaires looked out from the upper storeys of their mansions to their ships returning from the Caribbean, laden with cotton, sugar, tobacco. Nobody talked about how these goods were harvested. Rumours were thick – the God-fearing, the pious, the ones who knew nothing about business or how it worked, wanted the trade abolished. Well, for those fat, well-fed merchants living in their twelve-bedroom homes by the river, they cared not a fig for any of that. They'd fight tooth and nail to preserve their livelihood, one which brought in the cash and which gave men like Rooster a career in crime from which he could thrive.

Once in a while, along the winding path of his life, he would come across characters who were similar to him. Rough diamonds, hewn from the streets. Sometimes this would work to his advantage and he would enter into brief partnerships, but always these would end at some point. Rooster was a loner, trusting only himself. It was a philosophy that had stood the test of time; whilst many had fallen by the wayside, Rooster had survived. Perhaps he hadn't flourished, but he had always filled his belly and for a man in his line of business, that was paramount.

Sometimes, however, he crossed the paths of dangerous men. Men who wanted to deprive him of what he had gained. Then he had shown his true mettle. Rooster was a large and powerful individual, his great, hunched shoulders a knot of muscle, his gnarled fists efficient in delivering blows of considerable power. Not many wished to cross Rooster; those who did always paid the price. Some had paid the *ultimate* price.

Recently, times had grown hard. Nothing seemed to be coming his way. Then news reached him of an old house, on the outskirts of town, with the promise of a stash of gold hidden beneath its rafters. So, he'd hatched his plan and entrusted his two best boys in the caper, which he felt sure would bring him real rewards and, perhaps, a chance for retirement.

But that was days ago and he had seen neither sight nor sound of either of them since. This both angered and saddened him, the latter an unusual emotion for this man forged from the unfeeling world of crime. He'd trusted Bert, liked him, seeing in his sharp wits and simmering intelligence glimpses of his own self when he too was a little lad. Josh, a typical chancer, was not forged from the same base material. More of a follower than a leader. Bert now, he had promise. He might even take over the business one day. But now Bert had rebelled. That was the only possible conclusion he could bring to the situation. Using his considerable guile, Bert had somehow convinced Josh they could branch out alone and keep the treasure for themselves. Rooster shook his head, a sigh escaping from his cruel mouth. Bert... Such a disappointment.

As these thoughts grew, twisting around inside his mind, his fingers closed around the cheap necklace in his hand. Anger welled up from deep within. Betrayal was something he could never tolerate, most especially in someone he liked. It hurt him that Bert had done this. There might be another explanation, of course; he'd sent Josh out again to find him after the little brat had informed him of Bert's 'disappearance'. And then Josh, too, had gone, so the conclusion was clear – Bert had double-crossed him!

Squeezed in his palm, the cheap trinket suddenly shattered, tiny shards of gold, purple and white painted paste spattering over the table-top. Rooster threw himself back in his chair, snarling. Did he seriously consider Burt could do such a deplorable thing? Might there not be a more sinister reason behind the two boys disappearing? His eyes narrowed. Old Palin, the undertaker in Cleveland Street, had told him of the posters being put up all over town; of a man who was kidnapping boys. Could this fate have befallen his two lads? Or was the first explanation more likely? They'd taken the treasure for themselves and scarpered?

If they had, there really was only one thing to do.

A tiny sound behind him broke his thoughts. It might be a rat, but Rooster grew wary. Rats did not cause floorboards to sag and groan. Pulling out the eyepiece, he got to his feet and turned.

In the gloom, something lurked in the corner next to the door. It was difficult to make out what the shape was. It appeared hunched and small, but not as small as a boy. There was something else, too. An atmosphere of menace. Rooster had never felt anything quite like it before in his life. For the fleetest of moments, something akin to fear gripped him. Desperately, he reached inside his coat and the gnarled cosh he kept in his belt.

It was the last conscious move he ever made.

A sudden flash of steel cut through the murky blackness and a blow as powerful as a steam hammer hit him. A great fountain of blood burst from Rooster's throat. He knew he was dead even before he hit the ground, his life spewing out in great gouts from where the razor-sharp blade had cut deep through his jugular vein.

As his body went into spasm, a figure stepped over him, moving to the table. Frantic fingers picked through the collection of gems. Then a snarl of despair. Then nothing.

"Where is it?" rasped the voice. But the pawnbroker knew he was talking to himself. Rooster was already dead, a large cape of blood fanning out from behind his head, his lifeless eyes staring into oblivion.

The pawnbroker cursed loudly, and hefted his foot into the dead man's ribs. It was his own stupid fault, of course. He'd felt certain that the gems would be here and now that they weren't, he would have to try and find those damned children again. He had acted too hastily; he should have interrogated Rooster to make certain. But then, Rooster was not the sort of person to confront openly. No, this had been the best course. It was only a temporary setback.

Pulling off his hat, he sat down and rubbed his face, unconvinced by his reasoning. As he sat there alone, with the dead body of the once great Rooster at his feet, a calmness gradually settled over him. The ultimate prize was not so very far away now; he had successfully removed his most dangerous obstacle, so why fret? What were those children to him but a minor inconvenience? And the gentleman? A formidable adversary indeed. Judging by the way he moved and fought, he was a man of training and experience. An army man, perhaps. But a Rooster he was not. Rooster was a killer and now Rooster was dead. The gentleman... well, he was what he was – a gentle man. The next time they met, the outcome would be the same. He'd die. Nothing to worry about there.

The pawnbroker gave a little, cynical laugh and bent down to wipe the knife blade on Rooster's sleeve. Satisfied, he stood up, sliding the blade into its sheath under his armpit. A thin sneer cut across his cruel, ashen face. Time was on his side. He could wait. The children would appear at some point, and Josh would help him. Little Josh, a trusting fool, willing to do anything for a shilling or two. He'd run away like a whippet, but that was to be expected, given what the gentleman had done. Damn him. If he hadn't appeared when he had, the gems would be recovered by now and all would be well. But Josh, when he decided to turn up, would come good. He'd find them, find them all. And then the pawnbroker would have his revenge.

"Damn them all," he muttered. He positioned his broad-brimmed hat carefully upon his shaven head and slunk out of the filthy room that had been, up until so very recently, Rooster's home but was now his morgue.

Chapter Fourteen

Indecisions

Jamie sat absently stirring his spoon through his cornflakes, whilst in the kitchen his mum busied herself with tidying away cups and plates. The kitchen was always immaculate, but she nonetheless seemed to find plenty to do. Jamie envied the way she could occupy herself with the most mundane of things; she never complained, just got on with it, smiling to herself, sometimes humming a little tune. She seemed totally devoid of any concerns whatsoever, although this couldn't be the case. The kitchen was her means of escape, a place where she could forget about Dad, or at least try, for Jamie knew that she must miss him, at least sometimes.

Their life had never been what could be termed 'idyllic', but Jamie never suspected that beneath the façade of normal, family life, real unhappiness lurked. His parents rowed, but didn't everybody's? Then, about a year ago, the rows became much more aggressive. There were accusations, threats, screaming matches punctuated with swearing, the like of which Jamie had not even heard in the school playground. Mum cried a lot, but so did Dad. Jamie remembered blundering into the bathroom to find his dad sitting on the edge of the bath, sobbing like a little boy. He froze, not knowing what to do. Dad looked up and, through his tear-filled eyes, he stared at Jamie with the most pained expression he thought he had ever witnessed. Before any words were spoken, Jamie turned and fled, not daring to think what might have caused such devastating unhappiness.

Not long afterwards, the day arrived when he woke up to find Dad gone. A letter had been pushed under his pillow, and Jamie read it with half-comprehension. Something about 'impossibilities, lies and betrayals'. The essential part was that Dad had left. Jamie cried, great body-jerking sobs, so loud they brought his mother into the room. Sitting down next to him, she put her arms around him, holding him close. They didn't speak. That closeness, that depth of caring, was the most touching and heartfelt he'd ever known.

A hand suddenly touched his shoulder and he gave a start, turning to see his mum smiling down at him. "Penny for them."

Jamie looked back at his cornflakes. He hadn't taken a single spoonful. He took a deep breath. "Mum..." His voice trailed away, sounding very small.

She sat down, concern etched into her face. Taking his hand in hers, she squeezed it gently. "Jamie, whatever it is, you can tell me. I won't judge you, I promise. I'll just listen."

Jamie shook his head. "It's not a problem, Mum." He looked at her again, feeling strangely uncomfortable. He'd found that since Dad had left, he had the ability to talk to his mum about almost anything. Kids at school had got wind of this somehow, ribbed him about it, calling him 'Mummy's boy' and other, typical hurtful words. They thought of him as weird, or strange. The irony of it was, he actually *was* his mummy's boy! There were reasons for it, of course, but he wasn't about to explain them to anyone else. If they chose to accept him as a friend, they would do it unconditionally. Like Sarah. Like Tim. No one need know about his dad, his mum.

"I don't know..." he said, stumbling over words which refused to come, denying him the ability to articulate his fears. Sighing deeply, he let his chin drop to his chest.

"Just talk, Jamie," encouraged his mum gently, "just start speaking and you'll find the words."

He looked up, his eyes wet. "I had a dream again…" he squeezed her hand now, "but… but this one was so terrible. I dreamt I saw a man being murdered, Mum." His eyes locked on hers and she responded, reaching out to stroke his hair. His pain was evident. "It was the man who controlled Bert and Josh, and all the other boys. The man they called Rooster. He…"

Shaking his head, he bit down on his bottom lip and stood up, anger boiling over. "I'm sick of all this, sick of feeling like it's *me* being controlled. Why is this happening, Mum? These dreams, these feelings? Then Tim tells me he has the same dreams, and now he's gone missing…" He stopped, his voice trailing away as the realization of what he'd let slip hit him. His mum tensed and Jamie looked away from those wide, blazing eyes. He swallowed hard.

"You've spoken to him?" Now it was her turn to be angry. She shot to her feet, grabbed his shoulders and swung him round to face her. "I've asked you a question. Have you spoken to Tim?" She shook him and the tears rolled down his face. She stepped back. "But you told the police you hadn't… My God, you *lied* to them – and to me! What's happened to you, Jamie? It's like you're possessed or something – like you've become some sort of monster."

Her words stung him like blows to the face and he recoiled, wincing. "*No!*" he yelled. "I had to, don't you understand?" He could see she didn't, being too consumed by her own anger to make any sense of anything he said, but he plunged on regardless, his words pouring out of him unchecked.

"He wanted me to go to the house, and we did because we had to know the truth, to find out if our dreams were real. We're both having them, Mum. The same ones, over and over, and they're becoming more real, like we're actually living them ourselves. Oh Mum, Mum, *please…* It's these dreams making me this way.

I don't want to tell lies, but nobody would believe me if I told them the truth. The police, they'd just laugh, or think me crazy. I don't know, but I didn't do any of it on purpose. They come to me every night. I can't shut my eyes without seeing *him* – the pawnbroker. It was him who murdered Rooster, don't you see? And he wants to get Bert and Annabel, kill them, take the jewels they found in the house – the same house Tim and me went into. It's all real, Mum and it's awful and I'm scared."

"*You're* scared? What about me? Don't you think I've been through enough without all this nonsense? First you break into a house, then you stay out all night, now you lie to the police. The *police*, Jamie! That's a crime, don't you realize that?" She raked a hand through her hair and flopped down on a chair, suddenly looking very tired. "I can't take much more of this," she said quietly and put her face in her hands.

Jamie stood rigid, frozen to the spot, and watched her. This was how she'd been when Dad had first left. She'd sit and hide her face like this, sitting there for hours, not moving, hardly breathing, no tears, no sounds, just sitting. And now it was happening again, only this time it wasn't Dad's fault, it was his, Jamie's.

"Mum," he said, voice low, cautious, knowing how she could so quickly erupt, "Mum, I'm sorry. I didn't know what to do. I didn't mean to lie to you, or to anyone, but I couldn't tell you I'd been to the house again... you'd have killed me."

She looked up, her eyes without emotion, staring straight at him, "Oh, and this is better, is it?"

"No." He pulled a chair up close and sat down. He took her hands in his. She didn't flinch, which gave him the courage to continue. "We went to the house and Tim climbed the chimney, just like Bert did in my dream. He found jewels, a lot of jewels. He said he was going to get more, but that we should come home, which we did. He was... I don't know, he was just... oh, what's the word when you have to do something, no matter what?"

"Determined?"

"Yes, yes, that's it! He was *determined* to climb up the chimney again and get more of those jewels. There was nothing Sarah or I could say to stop him." His voice faded as he saw a new, even more outraged look crossing her face. He held his breath.

"*Sarah*? What, you mean you've got Sarah involved in all this nonsense, too?" Releasing a small, scoffing laugh, she stood up. "Well, this just gets better and better! I thought she was a little more grown up than that, to be honest. I thought that she was a sensible, *honest* girl."

"But she is, Mum. You know she is."

"Then why didn't she tell me what you were all planning? Why didn't she do the *honest* thing and tell me what you'd all been up to? I trusted you, Jamie. I let you go out and meet her and instead, you do this. You're all the same – the lot of you. I'm going back to bed." And with that, all discussion was at an end. Flying out of the room, she stomped up the stairs and slammed her bedroom door shut with a resounding crash.

Jamie sat and looked at his untouched cornflakes again. They seemed to reflect his feelings right now. A distasteful mess. What a disaster that was, a car wreck of a conversation if ever there was one. She hadn't listened to anything, hadn't even re-acted to the one thing he really wanted to tell her – that he'd witnessed Rooster's murder.

All of a sudden, he knew what he had to do. It would mean deceiving his mum yet again, but this time it might make all the difference to her accepting his stories as facts. Most importantly, it wouldn't involve anyone else. Hastily, he scribbled down a note and taped it to the television screen, checked he had enough change in his pocket, that his mobile was fully charged, then left the house at a jog, not daring to look back in case he found his mother's face pressed against her bedroom window, her mouth open in a scream of fury.

* * *

The librarian welcomed him with a beaming smile. "Hello again," she said. "Come to find out some more about Birkenhead in Victorian times? I hope you're going to turn your phone off this time!"

Jamie nodded and returned her smile. Although she looked very studious in her horn-rimmed glasses and tightly bunched hair, pulled back painfully from her face, she was actually quite nice looking and that made it very easy to spend time amongst dusty books and dog-eared maps.

"I'd like to look up some newspaper reports, please. Same period as last time."

She nodded slowly, "Okay… what are we looking for, exactly? More reports about missing boys? What was his name… Josh?"

His eyes met hers. "No, not this time. This time I need to know about a murder."

* * *

When he eventually got home, armed with the evidence that what he had seen in his dream really had happened, his mum was still in her room. Perhaps she hadn't even noticed him going out. Or perhaps she didn't care. Whatever the reason, Jamie wasn't bothered, not anymore. He had the proof and that was all he needed to convince her of his honesty. He pulled out the photocopied front page and laid it out flat on the kitchen table. There it was, the full report of the discovery of Rooster's body and a detailed description of what had happened to him. All that was missing was any suggestion of who the perpetrator was. But Jamie knew who that was, anyway.

Underneath the report was a biographical sketch of Rooster, his early life, his crimes. It was all there, every grisly detail. With keen interest, Jamie read it through for at least the sixth time until every word was ingrained in his memory. Strange how the authorities knew so much about him, yet never had any evidence to bring him to justice. He appeared immune. Jamie supposed that that was how most major villains managed to get away with their crimes – lack of proof. Rooster undoubtedly used intimidation and fear to keep possible witnesses silent. It was a tactic which worked extremely well, except, of course, against the one person for whom no amount of threat would ever work. The one person Rooster should have been most concerned about – his killer, the pawnbroker.

Chapter Fifteen

Spiral Downwards

During the next few weeks they spent with Mr Taylor, a brilliant transformation came over Bert and Annabel. No longer dishevelled, lost and without hope, their new home made them feel wanted, cared for and, for the first time in either of their small lives, there was a reason to go on. A future, a *real* future, now beckoned them and neither had any intention of letting the opportunity they had been given pass by.

The morning Mr Taylor called them both into what he referred to as 'the drawing room', they stood side by side, wide-eyed and anxious, gazing at the high ceiling from which hung a huge chandelier, noting the sumptuously upholstered furniture, the large paintings of faraway places on the walls. Neither spoke. Bert felt his heart thumping. Something was up, he just knew it.

Reading a letter, Mr Taylor seemed not to notice them at first. Bert arched an eyebrow towards the maid who had accompanied them to the room. She gave a tiny smile for an answer, mouthing, "wait". Sighing, Bert squeezed Annabel's hand.

At last, Taylor lowered the paper and settled his gaze upon Bert. "I've sent for someone."

Frowning, Bert tilted his head. "I'm sorry, sir? You've sent for someone to do what?" His grip on Annabel's hand tightened.

She shot him a frightened look. Had Mr Taylor succumbed to his suspicions, his sense of duty, and summoned the authorities, the Board of Guardians, to take them both away?

"If you're to make anything of yourself, Albert, then you must learn how to be a gentleman."

Stunned, Bert let out a short, sharp laugh. "A *gentleman*? Mr Taylor, sir, I'm no gentleman, nor am I ever likely to be."

"That's precisely why I've called for help. Miss Simmons is a teacher."

"What, letters and stuff?" Releasing Annabel's hand, he took a step backwards, bumping into the maid who tried to hold his arm. He yanked it free. "I'm not going to no board school, not now, not ever."

"She is a teacher of elocution. She is going to teach you your letters, yes, but not in a school. Here. In this room. This will be your study. You and Annabel – although," he turned a warm smile towards her, "I have the suspicion that you already know how to read, my dear. Is that true?"

Annabel curtsied. "Yes, sir. I can read and write. I know my numbers too, sir."

"I thought as much," said Mr Taylor.

Bert growled. "Well, that's all very well if you're used to all of that, but me, I'm too old. I can't do it – I *won't* do it!"

"If you're to stay here, then you must."

"Then I'll not stay."

Whirling around on her heels, Annabel looked horrified. "*Bert,* how can you say such a thing! If Mr Taylor is kind enough to offer you schooling, you should take it and not be so flaming ungrateful."

"I'm not ungrateful, it's just that I'm –"

"Yes, you are. Mr Taylor has given us a roof over our heads and fed us, clothed us with these lovely clothes and you … you're going to ruin everything!"

"No, I'm not, Annabel. I'm not, I promise, it's just that I'm –"

"You are, Bert!" Tears sprang from her eyes and she hastily grabbed at her sleeve, pulling out a small square of embroidered material to dab at her face. "Everything. Ruined." She sobbed.

Taking a step forward, Bert reached out his arms. "Annabel, please, don't cry. It'll be all right, I promise you it will."

"How can it be all right if you run away? And run away to where? Rooster, your old life? If that's what you want, then fine, do it. But I'll not go with you, Bert. I'll not."

"Annabel, please…"

"No, Bert. I'm happy here. You hear me? Happy. You're stupid and ridiculous, turning your back on Mr Taylor and everything he's given us. Too old? How can you be too old, you stupid, stubborn oaf!"

Bunching his fists, he brought them up to his face, a face reddening with barely contained fury. "I'm *not* stupid, I'm not!"

"Yes, you are, damn you."

"I'm *not – I'm just bloody well frightened, all right? Frightened!*"

Sometime later, sitting down sipping hot, sweet tea, Annabel's arm around his shoulders, Bert gradually calmed down. He'd wept, holding onto Annabel like he'd never let her go, and she'd stroked his head, telling him all would be well. All he had to do was try.

* * *

And try he did.

Miss Simmons proved to be a wonderful teacher and striking in appearance. Tall, elegant and, Bert had to admit despite her spectacles and hair pulled back so tightly from her face she appeared to be always on the verge of anger, very attractive. If anyone was going to give him lessons in reading, writing and the strange sounding subject of etiquette, it would be her. And he discovered, much to his surprise, how enjoyable it all was, even the constant repetition of incomprehensible chants such as, 'the rain in Spain falls mainly on the plain'. He'd do anything to please her.

"You like her, don't you, Bert?" commented Annabel one evening after class.

He blushed, but didn't answer. She laughed and he punched her playfully in the arm. "I like you more," he said at last. They both laughed at that.

Each day he looked forward to the lessons, and each day he gained in confidence and understanding. Soon, he was reading passages from books he never knew existed, lost in worlds created by great authors from the past. He loved it and wondered why he had ever felt such a fear of learning.

Not only did he develop his understanding of words and numbers, he learned to walk with a straight back, how to respond in the correct manner when meeting others of a certain class, how to conduct himself as a young gentleman, with grace, elegance and good manners. Strength of character. Assertiveness.

So when they next saw Josh, there was no struggle. No desire to run, or even to confront him. They were secure. Not even Josh could threaten them now. He was from a different world, one which was long gone.

Or at least that is what they believed.

* * *

The park had not changed that fateful day. Nor had Josh. Slinking through the town's backstreets, he returned to the pawnbroker, both of them licking their wounds. When the bell clanged above the door, announcing his arrival, he stood in the gloom and waited, breathing hard through his mouth, fear controlling him. Fear of what might happen if he stayed away and the pawnbroker hunted him down and killed him, and fear of returning to the punishment which he would undoubtedly receive.

"Where have you been, you snivelling wretch?"

He recoiled into the corner, hands coming up, surrendering, pleading, his voice whimpering, scared to death. "Please sir, I was terrified the Peelers would catch me. I didn't want to lead them straight back here."

The black shape loomed over him, the eyes peering out from the skull-face. Fingers wormed around Josh's throat and he gasped, preparing himself for the squeeze, the precursor to a lingering, painful death.

But the pressure remained slack.

"If you're lying to me, boy…"

"I'm not, sir. I promise. I wouldn't be here, would I, if I was."

"No. I suppose not." The fingers slipped away and Josh allowed himself a long, slow sigh. "Have you found them?"

"Not yet."

"I want you back out in the streets. I want you to hunt them down, you understand? I want to know where they are, where that bastard lives. The one who saved their miserable lives. I'll skin them all, do you hear me?"

The face thrust forward and Josh shrieked.

"I'll not suffer any such indignity again. No one betters me and lives. You believe me, boy?"

"Yes sir, I do, sir."

"Your former employer did not prove an obstacle, and neither shall that swaggering piece of slime who knocked me down."

Josh dragged a trembling hand across his face, a slab of ice developing in his guts. "Former employer, sir?"

"The one you called Rooster. I did for him, and I'll do for the rest of them. Now, get out and find them. And don't come back until you've got word of them."

Bobbing his head, Josh squeezed past and reached for the door. As his hand formed around the handle, the pawnbroker's fingers suddenly gripped him, ice-cold, and strong this time. Like steel. "You double-cross me, boy, and I'll slit your gizzard and dump you in the docks, you understand?"

Too terrified to speak, Josh could barely offer a whimper before the pawnbroker ripped open the door and shoved him out into the street.

For days, he skulked around Birkenhead Park, biding his time, feeling certain that they would reappear. His patience had been rewarded. Knowing Mr Taylor would eventually allow the young couple to stroll through the park, all Josh had to do was wait, despite the hunger gnawing away at his guts, the cold setting his teeth on edge, the rain in the night soaking him through as he cowered amongst bushes or underneath a park bench. The man was not their jailer, after all. He had to trust them at some point and, believing the danger was past, he would let them spend time in the park. They would have absolutely no intention of running away, or giving up what had been so graciously given to them. A home. A life. Things Josh never had.

So he waited. And then, at last, they came.

* * *

It was a brilliant afternoon, the sun beating down, the well-to-do out in their finest clothes, strolling along, parasols protecting them from the glare, noses upturned. Ladies in full, trailing dresses, men in top hats and tails. Bert and Annabel sat next to one of the lakes, tossing pieces of bread into the water, giggling as the ducks scrambled to catch the tiny morsels.

Josh sneered at their newfound self-confidence and stepped out from amongst the trees where he'd been hiding and watching. He strode towards them, noting that neither seemed afraid to see him again. As he stood, hands on hips, he ran his eyes over them both. Bert, dressed in a tweed jacket, with matching breeches tied under the knees, grey socks, highly polished shoes with silver buckles. Annabel, sky-blue dress, large, floppy hat and twirling parasol. They looked for all the world like a perfect, well-to-do couple, out for their 'daily constitutional', as he knew all those toffs called it. He half expected them to show some alarm at his sudden appearance. They didn't, almost as if they had been expecting him. Trying to look aggressive, he became increasingly riled at their casual air. "You look a right snobby fart, you do, Bertie, with your nose stuck up in the air like that. You won't be so cocky when I tell you my latest news," he snarled.

Bert – who, unbeknownst to Josh, was now addressed as Albert – merely smiled. "Josh, it's good to see you. How have you been?"

Blinking a few times, Josh took a moment and swallowed down his surprise, wrong-footed by his former partner-in-crime's changed attitude. "What are you talking with a plum in yer mouth for? You don't fool me with your fancy clothes and your fancy little girlfriend. Or your airs and graces."

"I'm not trying to fool you, Josh. Mine and Annabel's lives have changed, for the better. There's nothing you could say which would interest us, so please, if you're only here to threaten, go away. It is due to the memories I cherish of our past friendship that I haven't reported you to the authorities. But I will if you try and do anything."

"That's good of you, Mr Smarty." Checking that nobody was within hearing distance, Josh bent his body forward and said with quiet menace, "The pawnbroker, 'member him?" He noticed the flicker of interest on Bert's face. "Yeah, I thought you might. Well he's been kinda busy, see. Rooster. You know Rooster, don't you – old Cock-bird?"

For a moment, Bert's self-assurance wavered and he struggled to remain calm. "What about him?"

Josh grinned. "That caught your attention, eh? Well…" He licked dry lips, piling on the suspense. "He's dead."

Bert blinked. He looked at Annabel, who shrugged. "Couldn't have happened to a nicer man, so I hear." She smiled a superior smile.

Josh shook his head. "Poor darlings, you have no idea what's happening, have you?" He leaned closer. Bert's fists bunched. "Had his throat cut, he did. Imagine that. Rooster! The top of the pile, he was. Well, he ain't no more, that's for certain."

"You mean, he was murdered?" blurted out Annabel whilst Bert, stupefied, could only manage to gape.

"Clever one, you is," snarled Josh. "'Course he was murdered! But who was it that did it, eh?" He chuckled smugly to himself. "I'm sure you can try a little guess?"

Bert took Annabel's hand and made to stand up. "Come on, we're leaving."

But Josh was having none of it. With a violent shove of his hand, he pushed Bert back onto the bench. "What's the matter, Bertie boy? You've gone a terrible shade of grey."

In that one blinding moment, Bert forgot all about home comforts, talks about etiquette, Miss Simmons, the lessons. Rushing forward, he gripped Josh about the throat. Annabel could do nothing, such was Bert's anger. She watched as Bert rammed Josh hard up against the trunk of a nearby tree. "You listen to me, you weasel – you leave us alone, do you hear me? You tell that evil, twisted pawnbroker that if I ever see his face again I'll report him – and you! We've had enough. We've got a new life now and we want to live it without seeing the likes of you."

He pushed the little crook to the side with such force that Josh fell in a flapping heap to the ground. Before he could recover enough to say anything, the two turned away, hand in hand.

Roaring his rage, Josh charged. He had got the better of Bert once, and he'd do it again.

But this was not the Bert he knew. Swinging around in a tight arc, hips low, Bert's fist connected with the side of Josh's face with tremendous force, dumping him to the ground where he lay, stunned, the wind and the strength knocked out of him.

They then continued on their way.

Rubbing his face, Josh slowly got to his feet and dusted off his clothes. He watched them as they strode out of the main entrance to the park. He felt the swelling developing across his jaw and winced. He'd pay for that, would Bert. Next time. Smiling despite the pain, he looked around to check nobody had witnessed anything and, keeping his distance, he followed them.

* * *

Neither of the children wanted anything to eat. Mr Taylor sensed their unease, but he wasn't going to push for an explanation; at least not yet. He made his excuses and left them alone whilst he took what he said was, a 'turn around the grounds'.

When the door closed, Annabel quickly went to Bert's side. "What are we going to do?" she asked anxiously.

Bert sat with his elbows on the table, chewing his nails, staring out through the large windows towards the garden beyond. He could see Mr Taylor lazily making his way towards some azalea bushes. He watched their saviour bending down to study the flowers. "I don't know," he said at last.

Annabel rushed on. "Look," she said. "You warned him off. And you punched him so hard, like you were a prize fighter." She squeezed his forearm, the pride evident in her voice. "If I know anything of Josh, that will certainly be enough. I doubt if we'll see him again."

Bert looked at her. "But you don't know Josh, Annabel. Not really. I *do*. I lived and stole with him for nearly three years. I know what he's like. A coward, sly, take your last sixpence… all of that and worse. You saw what he was like in the park a few weeks ago… what he would have done to you."

"He was only threatening…"

"He was only waiting to be told to do it, Annabel. He would have cut your lovely face as if he were cutting up a piece of pie." Bert jerked to his feet. "This is never going to go away, Annabel. Not so long as that pawnbroker is around. He's so desperate to get his hands on the jewels, he'll do anything. I rue the day I ever went to that house. The pawnbroker... he murdered Rooster."

"But why would he do that? What reason would he have?"

"The jewels, it's all about the jewels! He knew that sooner or later, Rooster would have another go, send some others from his gang to the house to find the old lady's loot. He was a rival, and the pawnbroker removed him."

Annabel pushed her fist into her mouth, eyes wet and wide. "Bert, if Josh told us all that, knowing we would work it out –"

"– then it won't be long before the pawnbroker comes looking for us," he finished.

"All right, so all we have to do is keep away from the park. Josh doesn't know where we live. We're safe as long as we keep away from all the usual places, your old haunts."

She went up to him, holding onto his sleeve, tugging at him with every word she spoke, putting emphasis on each syllable, trying desperately to convince herself as well as him. "We have to, Bert, otherwise our whole world will be plunged back into a terrible daily fight for existence. We mustn't allow anyone to send us back to that – we *can't*. We can stay here and we can remain safe."

"That's where you're so wrong."

The two children froze in terror.

The voice belonged to Josh.

* * *

Annabel gave a piercing scream, her hands flying to her mouth. Stepping in front of her, Bert readied himself and rushed forward. But this time Josh was ready for him. Deftly stepping aside he threw out his leg, grabbing Bert by the lapels and, using his forward momentum, sent his old friend careering violently into a tall dresser. There was a sickening crack as Bert's head collided with the heavy piece of furniture. Sliding to his knees, head down, Bert groaned and Josh was on him like a wildcat, grabbing a clump of hair, yanking back his head with one hand whilst pummelling him repeatedly with his other fist.

Not knowing what to do, Annabel stood screaming over and over, hoping against hope that Mr Taylor would come in and stop the terrible scene unfolding before her.

The blows continued, each punch accompanied by Josh's words, forced out through clenched teeth. "I'll teach you... not... to try and... beat me. You're nothing... Bertie... Nothing. I'll teach... you... a lesson... you'll never... forget!"

With a tremendous splintering crash, Mr Taylor exploded into the room, almost tearing the door from its hinges. In an instant, he summed up the situation, saw Bert's bloody and bruised face and charged, swatting Josh to the ground as if he were an insect. The boy could do nothing, so fast and furious was the attack. Falling over, he writhed on the ground, panic-stricken.

Taylor took him by the collar and pinned him to the ground whilst his voice, hard and determined and barely under control, barked out a series of orders. "Annabel, get my house-keeper. Tell her to run to the police and bring an officer back here. Then get some water and do something for Bert's face. Hurry, girl!"

All the while Taylor held Josh, his breathing was heavy but controlled, a look of grim determination set across his cultured face. Josh knew this was the end and he started to blub, more at his own stupidity than at his predicament. "Oh please, sir, please don't hurt me, sir!" If only he'd gone straight back to the pawnbroker. What had he hoped to gain by trying to do every-thing himself? A reward, praise, what? And now... now it was all well and truly up the spout.

* * *

After an eternity of waiting, the police had arrived and had taken statements from everyone. The housemaid tended to Bert's cuts and bruises whilst he gave the details of his relationship with Rooster to a serious-looking policeman who carefully and methodically recorded everything, punctuating each statement with a tut of disapproval and a shake of the head. Finally, when everything had been double-checked, and the two accompanying uniformed men had taken a sullen and deflated Josh away, the officer in charge slapped his notebook shut and gave Bert a measured look.

"These jewels you say you found?"

Bert answered the policeman's gaze with a steady stare of his own. He had long since decided, in his own mind, that the only way forward was to tell the truth. "Yes, sir?"

"Valuable, you'd say?"

Bert shrugged his shoulders. "I would think so. Why else hide them?"

"Why else indeed." The policeman thought for a moment, chewing the end of his pencil. "I may have to visit the old lady myself, find out a little more."

Panicking, Bert brushed the housemaid aside and stood up, thrusting out his hands, pleading. "No, please sir, that wouldn't be right, would it? What I mean is, perhaps she doesn't know about them? The news might…" he grappled for the words whilst the policeman waited patiently for him to continue, "well, it might be too much for her, emotionally."

"Emotionally?" The policeman raised his eyebrows and turned to look at Mr Taylor. "You're educating this young man well, sir."

Taylor gave a proud smile. "Oh, I think anything he has learned has been down to his own efforts, officer." He placed a hand on the man's shoulder and gently guided him towards the door. "It may be," he began in a low voice, "that the boy has a point. This lady, for whatever reasons, has no knowledge, as far as I can tell, that the jewels actually exist. There must be a reason for that."

On reaching the door, Taylor opened it, gesturing for the policeman to step outside. It was a bright day, the warm sun bathing everything in a glorious light. They both breathed in the air. "Perhaps it would be more appropriate to guide the lady into contacting her lawyer. I feel sure there is a reason why this chest was hidden, and not simply because of its valuable contents."

The police officer nodded his head thoughtfully. "I do take on board what you say, sir, and I don't doubt that there is a very compelling reason why this chest has been concealed, but I can't help thinking that if it were lodged in a more secure place..." His voice trailed away and he looked out into the grounds of the house. "However, I think, on balance, that your suggestion is the best one, sir." He took Taylor's hand and shook it firmly. "Be assured, sir, I will suggest that the old lady speak to her lawyers, and let them help solve this conundrum."

He paused at the door and turned to give Taylor a meaningful look. He cleared his throat. "There have been reports of children going missing in this area, sir. I don't know if any of this is connected, and I'm sure you'll do this anyway, but don't allow your children out on their own. Not for a while, at least."

"Have no fear, officer. From now one, I won't let them out of my sight."

Smiling, the officer tipped his hat and walked away.

After watching him go, Taylor returned to the room to find Bert and Annabel sharing the same armchair, cuddling up close to one another, looking frightened. He smiled reassuringly and went over to them. "I think that things will only get better from this point. " He got down on his haunches and took each of their hands in his own. "You mustn't concern yourself too much. Josh is in custody and it won't be long before that pawnbroker is caught and put behind bars. It's over, children. Trust me."

Chapter Sixteen

Drink can Loosen the Tongue…

The gin house was a dank and dreary place, the few lit gas lamps unable to penetrate the gloom with their feeble, utterly inadequate light. In one particularly dark corner, the pawnbroker sat, features hidden by the brim of his hat. Even inside, he preferred people not to catch sight of his features. His was an unpopular and dangerous profession. Many hated him for what he did, his charging of excessive interest, the paltry offers of loans he'd make on good quality merchandise. In the past, some had tried to intimidate him, a few had attempted violence. No one had succeeded. In addition to the deliberate air of menace he created about him, he was also perfectly capable of the most extreme violence – to which Rooster could testify, if he were still alive. But the true secret of the pawnbroker's success, if that was what it was, was his anonymity. He worked alone, trusting no one else but himself.

Now, for the first time in his career, he had enlisted the help of another. Josh. And Josh had disappeared. His decision to use the boy thief was taken out of desperation, for he craved those jewels and wanted to get his hands on more. But this decision had proved foolish. He'd been double-crossed and would have to rely on his own considerable abilities to achieve the goal he'd set himself – to take the treasure for himself, every last sparkling bauble of it.

A deep growl rumbled from his throat as his thoughts settled on Josh. He reached for the glass of gin at his elbow and drained it in one. He'd made a mistake, entrusting someone with a job he should have done himself. If he'd been more patient, he could have found those damned children himself. But here he was, idling away his time when those gems should have been helping him towards a new and better life. He hated this damned town, with its mass of poor, unwashed humanity, its lack of hope. Misery and despair were etched into every brick in every wall. The stench of it clung to his clothes like a second skin. The jewels, the treasure, were his ticket to a different, cleaner, brighter world.

Damn Josh and damn those bloody damned children!

He slammed the glass down on the table and almost at once a serving girl refilled it. She'd come from nowhere and he was a little startled, but also intrigued. He looked up at her. Beyond her grimy hands and streaked face where the make-up had been repeatedly applied without being washed off in between, she had a certain something. An undoubted attractiveness. Leaning forward, he touched her hand and leered. She recoiled instantly, as if stung.

"You keep your hands to yourself," she spat. "I'm not some bloody floozy, you know."

"Oh, now then, sweetie," he cooed, doing his best to sound pleasant, "I'll pay you well for your time. You should mind your manners when you have a customer willing to spend his money."

"I've manners enough for the right client – but that ain't you!" Tossing her head in exaggerated indignation, she whirled away and flounced off to other customers in other dark corners, leaving the pawnbroker to watch her, desire stirring in his loins. He sat back, sniggering, and drained his glass in one. "More gin, you bitch!" he cried out, causing those within earshot to turn and look at him with alarm.

The girl scowled at him, torn between carrying out her duties and the revulsion she felt at being so close to such a creature. He filled her with loathing, not just for his profession but for his very physical presence. She'd never encountered anyone so lewd and sickening in temperament and demeanour.

A sudden bark rang out across the crowded room. The owner of the establishment, a large, bullish individual ensconced behind the bar, shook his fist in her general direction. "Serve the customers, Daisy. Do your bloody job."

Shooting him a look, Daisy muttered her apologies to the men at the table she was serving and slowly approached the pawn-broker with a growing feeling of dread.

She could see him watching her intently, a sneer etched across his thin, gaunt face. When she reached his side, he leaned forward again, running his tongue across his bottom lip. "Seems you're not doing your duty, sweetie."

She glowered, the sight of him almost causing her to gag. He was a loathsome, vile creature, spawned from slime, twisted and grotesque, forged in some underground cavern where no light or humanity could penetrate. She shuddered as his thin fingers, like slimy, oily eels, folded around her own. Squeezing her eyes shut, she forced herself to suffer the cold wetness of his touch without flinching.

"That's better, sweetie," he hissed, taking the newly-filled glass of gin from her grasp and raising it to his blue lips. "A toast," he cackled, "to us!"

He threw back the drink, then gripped her hand and brought it to his lips. She yelped and pulled back from his grip, shouting out, "There's no 'us' – not now, not ever!"

"Oi!"

The shout of the owner boomed across the room. Conversations died away and a strange, preternatural calm settled over the place. All eyes turned to the man's great bulk looming out of the gloom. Steaming with anger, he dashed away a rickety chair in his path, and jabbed a finger at the pawnbroker. "What the 'ell's goin' on 'ere?"

"It's 'im," Daisy squealed, "touchin' me up and the like. He tried to kiss my bleedin' hand! I'll not 'ave it, you 'ear, I'll not. I'm a barmaid, not a floozy."

Sitting back, arms folded across his chest, the pawnbroker watched this little sideshow with growing amusement. It had been a while since he had such fun and he was enjoying himself. "I only offered her my hospitality," he said smoothly, taking a delicate sip from his glass. "Sorry if I offended."

"It wasn't 'ospitality you was offerin'," she spat. "You know full well what you was offerin' and I'm here to tell you I don't do any of that!"

He shrugged his thin shoulders and smiled back at her, "Well, no harm done," he took another sip, pausing for effect, "sweetie."

She threw her bar-towel at him and flounced off, tossing her hair in anger.

"We don't offer that type of service 'ere, sir," said the owner. "If it's that sort of thing you want, I suggest you go elsewhere."

The pawnbroker raised his glass towards the owner. "My thanks to you, dear man, for enlightening me."

A silence descended over the two men, the owner measuring this strange customer carefully. There was something about him he didn't like. Having been in the trade for all of his life, he prided himself on being a very good judge of character. Crooks, thieves, swindlers and braggarts, he knew them all; but this one was different. Dangerous he was, like a coiled cat ready to spring. He took an involuntary step back as the pawnbroker continued to stare.

"I'll be grateful if you'd leave, sir," he said slowly, "as soon as you've finished your drink."

The pawnbroker raised one eyebrow, looked at his glass, drained it in one, then stood up, pushing his chair back loudly. The owner sucked in a breath, preparing himself for violence.

"There," the pawnbroker said, tossing a handful of coins dismissively onto the table, "all finished." He tipped the brim of his hat and turned to make his way out.

"And I'd appreciate it if you didn't come back, sir," the owner said to the man's back.

The pawnbroker stopped for a moment, pulling up the collar of his coat, then turned very slowly, his glare piercing the grey, stinking air. "I go where I please, publican."

Sensing the crackling tension in the atmosphere, the nearest customers started inching away. Others waited. No one moved.

Knowing his reputation depended on what happened next, the owner could not afford to back down. He ran a profitable business and the many villains who frequented his place rarely caused trouble, for they all knew what the consequences were. The owner's name rang out across the plaque above his door. Victor Marshall, ex-prize-fighter, renowned for his left hook and ability to take a punch. Drink had been his downfall, not another man's fists. He rarely needed to rely on his old skills anymore, but could dish it out just as well as he ever could. Few, if any, ever wished to take a blow from his sledge-hammer fists.

Sighing deeply, Marshall stepped forward, deciding to eject this loathsome individual. "Come on you, you're out on your arse!"

The pawnbroker didn't move, just watched the big man come on with an air of detached indifference. Overconfident, Marshall's sheer size usually enough to overcome an opponent, his great hands came up, bunched into fists. The pawnbroker smiled.

Witnesses later told the police that Marshall never landed a single blow; that the pawnbroker simply danced to one side, the blade of his knife sinking deep into Marshall's throat. A powerful wrench sliced through veins and ligaments and before the big man fell to the ground, the pawnbroker had gone, a great flourish of his coat concealing the direction he took. In the commotion that ensued, with many attempting to stem the flow of blood with towels and coats or anything else that came to hand, no one dared follow the assailant into the busy streets and find out where he went to.

He disappeared as mysteriously as he had arrived, nameless and faceless, leaving his trademark of death behind him.

Chapter Seventeen

A Chance Encounter?

Jamie had been sitting up in bed for quite a while when his mum came in with some tea and toast. She smiled and placed the breakfast tray across his knees. "Peace offering," she said quietly and stepped back to look at him closely. "Thank you for leaving your note."

"You're not mad?"

A little shrug. "I was, but… I'm *trying* to understand. Did you have another bad night?"

He nodded his head and tentatively picked up a piece of toast. "It's every time I close my eyes now." He took a bite and munched on it half-heartedly. "I'm almost afraid to go to sleep."

She sat down beside him and ruffled his hair, giving her best, reassuring smile. "It'll be all right."

"You think?"

"Perhaps we should see a doctor?"

Jamie stopped in mid-bite and glared at her. "Why? I'm going mad, is that it?"

"No, of course not, it's just –"

"You don't believe *any* of it, do you?"

She looked at him for a long time, not really knowing how to continue. Then she pulled back and wiped her hands on the apron she was wearing. "I believe *you* believe it, Jamie. That's the important thing."

Sucking in his bottom lip, he thought for a moment before carefully placing his half-eaten piece of toast on the plate. "So, if I can get some shrink to talk to me, this might all stop?"

She sensed his anger and stood up. "I don't suppose you'll be wanting any of this now," was her parting shot as she took the tray away.

He watched her go, determined not to allow his anger to take control. In a strange way, he appreciated how she felt. How could *any* of it be real? He got up and pulled on his clothes. Crossing to his computer, he jiggled the mouse and the screen came alive. He had an e-mail waiting and when he saw it was from the Reference Library, all his anger disappeared. Feverishly, he opened it and began to read its contents.

The librarian had found another newspaper report, dated some weeks after the first. It detailed how the police had been questioning two young people and had taken a third into 'protective custody'. She'd scanned in the report and attached it to the message.

After he'd read through the newspaper report for the second time, he sent an e-mail to the librarian thanking her, then a second to Sarah. He felt certain now that the answers were in his grasp. Everything seemed to be accelerating towards some sort of conclusion, but he still needed Sarah's help. When it came to local history, Sarah had proved herself to be the best there was at school. If anybody could tie all the threads together, it was she.

Now came the waiting. He knew he could have phoned her, but that would probably mean having to talk to her mum, and that he just didn't want. He still felt unsure about the whole *relationship* thing. God, how he hated that word, but he so wanted them to have exactly that – something more than mere friendship But how could he be sure if she *really* liked him? Maybe she had some weird sort of crush on him? When she'd told him he was 'interesting', he'd dismissed it out of hand, but perhaps it was true. He didn't know. What he *did* know was that he definitely had a crush on her! But how could reveal his feelings without scaring her off?

He sat back and again studied the email he'd composed. Should he send her another message to tell her of his feelings? That he thought about her all the time? That the day they'd spent together was the best ever? Wouldn't she simply laugh at him and wave him goodbye?

After all, she was a girl and girls were never easy to talk to, especially about really serious stuff. And besides...

His e-mail alert pinged. There she was, almost as if they'd made a kind of mental connection! He scrambled to open her message and read it through breathlessly, not daring to believe her words. But there they were, big and bold, asking him to meet her at the library tomorrow afternoon. He gazed at the words through glazed eyes. She had *actually* written – *Text me to confirm the date!* His cheeks burned as his fingers hovered over the keyboard, preparing to give her his reply.

Then he stopped.

Mum would have to okay it all first. After this morning's little blow-up, he wasn't sure if she would. He was still, officially, grounded. Mum had been lenient in the past, but now... He slowly made his way downstairs, each step taking him deeper and deeper into despair. She was bound to say 'no'.

She was in the kitchen, doing what she did best – making bread. He always marvelled at her ability to make the most perfect soft-rolls, baguettes, loaves, or just about anything else. He stood in the entrance, watching her. If she knew he was there, she didn't show it, continuing to knead the dough with a grim determination.

After a short while, he cleared his throat and she shot him a glance, the anger clear on her face. He tried a smile. "Mum,

I know you were only trying to help. I'm sorry for the way I reacted."

Wiping her hands on her apron, she cocked her head and smiled back. "What do you want?"

"Huh?"

"You're after something, what is it? "

Knowing it was hopeless to try to fool her, he shrugged and stepped closer, hands spread out, his voice pleading. "Mum, *please,* Sarah's just got in touch…"

"Oh. I see," she placed the finished bread into a tin and covered it with a cloth, "and you'd like to go and meet up, is that it?"

He couldn't hide his surprise. "How did you know?"

She looked at him over her shoulder, "I'm your mother. You should know by now that you can't hide anything from me."

That made him smile. The atmosphere thawed and he stepped closer still. "It's not until tomorrow. I'll go on my bike. I won't be home late but if I am, I'll text you."

"Today you've got something else to do." She leaned back against the table edge, arms folded. "Have you spoken to Tim?"

Jamie blinked and did a double-take. He hadn't thought about Tim at all and this realisation made him suddenly feel guilty. "No." He looked at her, then added for effect, "I'm not allowed."

His words had no outward affect. If they stung her, she didn't show it. "His mum's been on. She's very worried about him. She wants you to phone her."

"Me? Why?"

She stared. "Because he still hasn't come home. She phoned me this morning, before you woke up. I don't know her that well, but she sounded desperate. She just wanted to ask you a few things."

"Like what?"

"She wouldn't say. I think she's been going through the same things with him as I have with you…" Her voice trailed away, and she looked embarrassed. "Sorry," she said quickly, "I didn't mean it like that. You know what I mean."

Jamie nodded. "Yes, I do." He smiled, reached forward and squeezed her arm. "I'll go and ring her now."

* * *

He replaced the receiver slowly. Tim's mum *had* sounded desperate. Did he have any clue about where he might have gone, and why? Had he been in touch, a text, a note, anything? But there was nothing he could offer by way of reassurance. "He told me about dreams," she said. "A man with sharp features, a wide hat and huge, black cloak coming towards him in the night. Do you know who he is, Jamie? What he wants? Is any of it real, or is it a figment of Tim's over-active imagination?"

"I don't know," he lied, feeling helpless. When he heard her sob, his heart lurched. He took a breath and was about to say something when the phone went dead.

He gaped at the receiver. Why would she simply hang up like that?

"Oh, dear God," he heard his mum shout. She appeared from the kitchen and opened the under-stairs cupboard. "The damned electricity has tripped."

Racing upstairs, he found his computer frozen. All the power in the house was down. There was no way of knowing if Sarah would meet him at the library or not. Worse still, there was now no way to tell Tim's mum that the man with the sharp features and the black hat *was* real. Because he was. Jamie knew this for certain. He was not simply a character in a dream.

He slumped down on his bed. Why had this happened now, of all times? They *never* had power cuts!

The front door opened and closed.

He listened out for his mum. Did she never, ever, just do *nothing*?

After a few minutes, the door opened again and he heard her muttering to herself. She called up to him, "I went next door and talk to Mrs Roberts. The whole street is down. Apparently, they're doing something with the supply down in the town. We'll be without electricity until lunchtime." She paused, took a deep breath. "If you've nothing to do, you can go and put out the rubbish, then go down to Jimmy's for some more bin-bags."

Reluctantly, he went downstairs. She pulled a couple of coins from her pocket and thrust them into his hand. "You can get yourself a bar of chocolate with the change, if you want."

He took the money and went out, dutifully putting the black plastic bag of rubbish into the large bin standing at the side of his house. Then he walked down his quiet street to the corner. He rounded it and stared ahead towards the sign above Jimmy's shop. But it wasn't Jimmy who Jamie saw standing in the shop doorway.

Quickly, before the hawkish-looking man in a large black coat and black hat caught sight of him, he dipped into another shop doorway and waited, taking in air in great gulps. He felt sure the man hadn't seen him. Carefully now, Jamie slid down to one knee and peered from his hiding place to take in his features. As he looked, icy-cold fingers tickled the back of his neck. There could be no doubt. No doubt at all.

The shop door suddenly opened with a loud jolt and Jamie yelped, spinning around to see the owner glaring down at him. "What the bloody hell are you up to? Bloody kids. Get the hell away from my door, you bloody nuisance!"

Not waiting to argue, Jamie turned and ran back home. He didn't dare look back until he reached his own front door. A quick look reassured him he hadn't been followed, then he blasted his way through the front door and took the stairs two at a time before his mum could ask him what was wrong. He just had time to shout down to her that the shop didn't have any more bin-bags, before he plunged into his room and slammed the door behind him. He stood with his back to the door, breathing heavily, not daring to believe what he had just seen. But the more he thought about it, the more he knew. It was him. The pawnbroker! Who else could it have been? That face, those clothes?

But how could it be? The whole thing was senseless. People in dreams aren't real. People from the past aren't real. His imagination was to blame. Talking to Tim's mum, the coincidence of the electricity blowing just as he was about to tell her... tell her about the pawnbroker.

Feeling a little calmer, he crossed his room and, hiding behind the curtain, took a peek outside. There was no one around. Breathing a deep sigh of relief, he flopped down onto his bed. Imagination or not, he wouldn't be going out of this house again that day, that was for sure.

Chapter Eighteen

An Unwanted Visit

The news had reached the household earlier that morning and already Taylor was making preparations. Josh had managed to escape from police custody. The Inspector had come to deliver the news personally. "I do not seriously believe the boy will return to your house, sir," he said, standing in the hallway, holding his hat in both hands moving the brim through his fingers, "but if he has once again fallen into the evil clutches of the pawnbroker, then anything might be possible. I'm sorry I can't be any more specific, sir, but we're dealing with dangerous and desperate people. People who are capable of anything."

"So what do you suggest, Inspector?"

"I could put a man outside, sir. As a sort of deterrent."

"You think that will work?"

A pained expression crossed the police officer's face. "Of that, I couldn't actually say, sir. I'm sorry."

After showing the inspector out, Taylor instructed his housekeeper to pack overnight bags for himself and the children. "It is my intention, Mrs Delaney, to leave for a few days and go and stay with my sister in Bristol. I took the precaution of sending her a telegram in order to forewarn her. It seems I was right to do so."

"I'll run along to the butcher's and buy some cold meat to make sandwiches for the journey, sir. I'll then go on my weekly visit to my own sister. I'll lock the house up before I leave. Hopefully, the police constable they send will have his wits about him and keep a good eye out."

Taylor said nothing to the children of his plans and they remained in ignorance for the rest of that day, playfully chasing each other in the ornamental gardens whilst he busied himself with his daily correspondence. It was a beautiful day and he had opened the porch windows so that he could hear their voices as they played.

He was in the middle of his second letter when he heard the first piercing scream. Taylor whirled around to see his two young wards running frantically towards him across the grass. Behind them was the reason for their flight – Josh. The despicable knave had the audacity to come straight to the house, having escaped from the clutches of the police. How dare he! This was too much! The authorities would have to do better than this. Grabbing his cane, Taylor rushed towards the open porch.

* * *

Bert ran as if in a dream, Annabel clutching his shirt-tails, screeching in terror. Shooting a glance behind them, Bert saw Josh pumping his arms, teeth clenched in his wild face, relentless in his pursuit.

As he turned to look towards the house, he saw a sight that chilled his soul.

Stepping out from his study, Mr Taylor had been about to come to their aid once more, just as he had in the park, only this time the tables were turned. The pawnbroker must have been waiting, biding his time. He loomed up behind Mr Taylor and struck him an awful blow across the back of the head with an evil-looking piece of gnarled wood. Only one blow, but it was enough. Without a sound, Mr Taylor crumpled to the ground and lay motionless where he fell.

Bert and Annabel stopped dead in their tracks, their laboured breathing pounding in their chests. Annabel whimpered and gripped Bert's shirt fiercely. He put his arm around her and drew her close.

The pawnbroker slowly approached, a sickly smile cutting across his face; a smile of triumph. He idly tossed the piece of wood away and reached inside his coat to produce a long, thin-bladed knife. His smile turned to a grin.

Bert drew a deep breath. He knew, despite the fear gripping him, that he wouldn't give up lightly. If he could give himself and Annabel some time, then perhaps Mrs Delaney would re-turn… But when?

Then he remembered she had taken the afternoon off to visit her sister. He squeezed his eyes shut, trying to block out the nightmare that was threatening to overwhelm him.

When he opened his eyes again, it was to discover that the nightmare was about to begin.

The pawnbroker stood before them.

He spoke evenly and quietly, which lent his voice a far more sinister tone than ever before. "We meet again. All thanks to Josh seeking you out. He's my little angel, he is."

Josh stepped up beside the pawnbroker, beaming with pride. "Thank you, guv. I did as you asked. It was easy. Almost as easy as getting away from the Peelers." He jutted his chin towards Bert, shaking his head in mock disappointment. "You've lost your street ways, Bertie old son, gone soft in the 'ead, you have. I couldn't have followed you a month ago."

Bert stared but didn't speak. The pawnbroker tutted. "Now, now, Josh. Don't cause him distress." He levelled his gaze on Bert and absently ran his thumb along the knife-blade. "What we have here, Bertie, is a situation. You see, I want the jewels, *all* the jewels, and you are the little gift horse who is going to get them for me."

"You're mad," spat Bert. "Why don't you get Josh to do it? He knows the house. Use him, and leave us alone."

The pawnbroker smiled even more broadly. "Ah, well, you see, that's just what I can't do. When you went back to the old lady, to return those few valuables you had to her... yes, that's right, I know all about it... well, you struck up quite a little friendship with her, did you not? Had her making cups of tea for you, eh?" He looked at Josh. "Not the sort of welcome poor Josh would get. Probably a clip round the ear, more like."

Josh laughed. The pawnbroker didn't. "No, what I'd like you to do, Bertie, is to pay the dear old soul another visit – she trusts you, silly old fool that she is – you and the lovely Annabel here. Yes, that's right, the pair of you can go and see her. And whilst Annie keeps the old dearie occupied, you can slip out, grab the jewels and pass them to me through the window."

"But if you know where they are, why can't you just break in? I told you, don't you remember?"

Sighing deeply, the pawnbroker shook his head. "Problem is, that was all a lie, wasn't it? You see, I did just that. Broke in, found the statue... but, would you believe it, no hidden compartment and no lovely lolly." A dry, humourless cackle. "No, you lied to me, little Bertie, and I don't like that. And that's why this time, we'll do things the proper way. Just like I've explained."

"And what if I won't do it? What if I refuse?"

"Then I'd be left with only one choice." His smile faded and his voice grew harder as he pointed with the knife. "You refuse, laddie, and I'll put little Annie here into the ground for good!"

Annabel gave another whimper and clung onto Bert's sleeve with every ounce of her strength. Bert could only smooth her hair. He knew there was nothing he could do except go along with the horrible man's plan.

Just then, like a voice of heavenly salvation, Mrs Taylor called from a high window.

Every face turned towards the sound.

Pushing open the window, she leaned out, caught sight of her husband's prone body, and let out a single piercing scream. It was enough to cause Josh to turn and immediately make ready his escape. But before he could take a step, the pawnbroker caught him by the collar and yanked him back to his side. "Hold on, Josh my lad." He turned a face flushed with rage towards Bert and glared.

It was a look that Bert would carry with him for the rest of his life.

"You haven't heard the last of me," snarled the pawnbroker. "I'll have that treasure, no matter what it takes!" Turning his attention Josh, his eyes slowly narrowed. "You should've told me about that woman, Josh, my boy. Now I'll have to reconsider me tactics."

Josh struggled to get free but it was hopeless. "She keeps herself to herself... I didn't know she was here, I swear."

The pawnbroker shook his head. "Not good enough. You let me down. I won't be let down by anyone." With frightening speed, he sank the blade into Josh's gut right up to the hilt.

A look of utter disbelief crossed poor Josh's face. He held onto the man's arm, eyes pleading. A violent shove and the blade went deeper still. Josh groaned, the pawnbroker laughed and, high above them, Mrs Taylor screamed again.

Knees buckling, Josh sagged, the weight of his body allowing the knife to slip free of his flesh as he pitched backwards onto the grass, the blood belching out of the horrific wound in his stomach. He lay there, staring skywards, eyes wide in fear as the colour drained from his face, giving him the appearance of a porcelain doll. From somewhere, he managed to find the strength to roll over and stand up. Gripping his stomach, he teetered towards a small ornamental pond some feet away. With one arm outstretched, he gripped the edge of the fountain and turned.

Annabel buried her face into Bert's shirt front. All Bert could do was stare. Something passed between them. Josh's lips curled into a thin, colourless smile. "Tell my mother…" he said, but then his eyes rolled up into his head and he tilted backwards into the water with barely a splash. He lay quite still, his eyes no longer registering anything at all, whilst around him the water turned a ghastly shade of pink.

Another scream broke the cold, dreadful silence. Whirling around, the pawnbroker sent a withering look towards Mrs Taylor, then wiped the blade of his knife across his sleeve and adjusted the angle of his hat.

From over by the porch doors, Taylor let out a low groan and sat up, pressing a hand against the back of his head. Grimacing in pain, he attempted to fix his dazed eyes on what was happening ahead of him.

Bert and Annabel took a tentative step towards the house.

"I'm not finished with you by a long chalk," spat the pawnbroker. He swept his voluminous cloak around him, and slunk off into the distance.

Chapter Nineteen

The Past Revealed

Jamie sat bolt upright in bed, his heart pounding so hard he was afraid it would burst out of his chest. He ran a quivering hand over his face. His entire body trembled. The nightmare, if that was what it was, had seemed as real as if he were witnessing an actual event. He sat still for a moment, trying to regain his bearings, then slowly got up out of bed and crossed over to his window. He scanned the many houses that surrounded his; the back gardens, the alleyways. They appeared the same as they always did. Quiet houses in quiet streets. Not at all like the ones in his dreams, which had huddled together in and around Hamilton Square.

In the dream, he'd visited the library and rooted out the records which told him that over a hundred years ago, the back streets were littered with pawnbrokers and moneylenders, squeezed in between grimy gin-houses and dens of iniquity. He'd set out to search those long-forgotten streets, and he'd found it, the very place. He'd recognised it instantly, a dream within a dream, or nightmares which were becoming increasingly more vivid and frightening. In a swirl of fog, he'd stopped short of entering what was essentially an empty shell of a building. He'd had neither the inclination, nor indeed the courage, to look further. And then he'd heard the voices and he'd turned and fled, not stopping until he came to the house again.

The house where he'd seen Josh die.

How much of it was real and how much a dream? He didn't think he could tell the difference anymore.

Sarah had said she'd help, so he ran down the stairs and called her number on the land line, his mobile having run out of charge.

Tapping his foot impatiently, he suddenly realised he had not checked the time. He guessed it was early morning, but perhaps it was *too* early. If her dad answered, he'd be in trouble. He had just decided to replace the receiver when a husky voice, thick with sleep, answered.

Taking a breath, Jamie identified himself.

The atmosphere crackled with tension. He could feel it filtering down the line.

And then the shouts. "Have you any idea what bloody time it is? It's quarter-past five in the morning!"

"I'm sorry, Mister –"

"What is it you want?"

Closing his eyes to weather the storm, Jamie took a couple of breaths. "I'm really sorry, but you see, I'd planned to meet Sarah this morning, as soon as the library opens. I'm just checking to make sure she hasn't forgotten. Could you pass on the message? Please?"

"Next time, you make your arrangements at a decent hour," and then the phone went dead.

* * *

At the breakfast table, the news was grave. Mum sat opposite him, chin propped in her upturned hands. "She telephoned again. Tim still hasn't turned up. The police have searched the old house and found nothing. Not even his bike, which is also missing. She was on the verge of hysteria when she rang off."

Jamie ate his cereal in silence. He felt so guilty. If only he had stopped Tim from going back to find more of those damn jewels. That house… It held some form of irresistible force, luring them ever deeper into its secrets. He hated it.

The minute hand of the huge wall clock crawled towards nine o'clock. From across the road, Jamie watched it, desperately wishing for the appointed hour to strike. When it did, the doors opened, and those other people waiting outside, armed with piles of books, trickled inside, but Jamie waited.

And waited. Sarah was late.

At twelve minutes past nine she finally appeared, sprinting around the corner.

"Where have you been?" demanded Jamie.

She stared at him, huffing crossly. "You what? You get my dad out of bed at five in the morning, to tell him something I already knew and –"

Jamie held up his hand. "All right, I'm sorry. I'm sorry. I really am. But I had to get you here as quickly as possible. I've got a plan."

Jamie explained his 'plan' as they went up the wide stone steps to the Reference Library.

"The maps you used to find the old streets are only one tool we can use," explained Sarah, revealing that special knowledge which made her such a source of envy at school. "We can check out every census taken of the street. They'll tell us the names of families and other people who lived in a particular place at the time the record was made. They also tell us their age and, more importantly, what they did for a job."

"I think I found out where his house is."

"You did? How?

"I went there." They walked into the hushed atmosphere of the Reference Library. Large oak tables were neatly laid in rows for people to study at. He leaned into her, pressing his lips against her ear. "I saw it. In a dream."

Her eyes stared back at him, flat and unblinking. He couldn't be certain if she believed him or not. Until she squeezed his hand and he almost swooned at her touch.

"We can find out if it's real, Jamie, because," she continued in a whisper, "the other thing we have is a street directory. That can tell you the whole history of a street, if you're lucky. And we, Jamie, are very lucky. Because we live here, in Merseyside, we have *Gore's* and *Kelly's*. And those two Street Directories should tell us what we want to know."

Jamie raised his hand in a silent greeting to the librarian, who returned his wave with a broad smile. Sarah raised an eyebrow and shot him a questioning look. Jamie shrugged his shoulders. "I've been here quite a lot," he said, in a hushed tone. "The lady over there helped me. I've looked at the Street Directories and the Census already." He turned his eyes down as she glared at him. "Like I said, I've also looked at some maps."

"So, you just let me rabbit on, like some idiot, explaining what everything is? Why didn't you tell me?"

He shrugged and offered her a half-smile, "Well, to be honest... because I really like the way you talk... all teacher-like."

She punched him in the arm. "You idiot!" But when she sat down at one of the tables, she was smiling. "So, what are we doing here then?"

"We're going to check the Directories again, looking for the names of pawnbrokers who had offices in and around Hamilton Square. I'll know the name."

"How will you know the name?"

"I told you – because of my dreams."

* * *

They worked all morning, using the copies of the census on microfiche and the original street directories. Immersed in their research, the time simply vanished and when they finally looked up, stretched their limbs and looked at the notes they'd taken, some three hours had flashed by. But not only had they discovered the address of the pawnbroker himself, they'd also built-up a detailed picture of the history of the street Jamie was after – the street in which Mr Taylor's house had once stood.

"It's all here," said Sarah, checking off the dates. "In the directory, for 1871, it's got Taylor, John, cotton merchant, and his address as Number 1, Mill Lane. Then," she picked up the photocopy of the census, "here we have him again – John G. Taylor, Head of family. Age last birthday, 37, rank, profession or occupation: cotton merchant; where born: Cheshire, Wallasey. Address is the same." She looked up and smiled. "The man in your dreams, the man who saved Bert. He's real, Jamie! It's all here."

Jamie chewed at his bottom lip, not yet convinced. "Can we be sure it's him?"

Sarah pushed over the papers. "There is no one else. Look at the directory. In 1871, there were only half a dozen people living in Mill Lane. No one else fits. It has to be him." Her finger stabbed at the page. "And look, Jamie, look at the entry for the names of the 'scholars'."

"*Scholars?*"

"All children of school-age were called scholars. Albert and Annabel. Jamie… it's them!"

He ran his hand through his hair. "My God! You mean…" He sat back, one hand clamped to his jaw, struggling to hold back the tears. "If this is all true, then my dreams… It's what you said, isn't it? They're a –"

"A portal to past events. Yes, that's exactly what they are, Jamie. I never seriously doubted you, you know."

"You didn't? But it's all so freaky! How can we be sure if the house I dreamt about is truly this one?"

"The names, Jamie. They're the same. There isn't any doubt, at least not in my mind."

"I know… I'm just feeling weird… this is all coming together so neatly. I feel really frightened, Sarah." As he lowered his head onto his crossed arms, she gently put her arm around him.

"It'll be all right, Jamie. Honestly. We've nearly cracked it, and when we finally have, I'm sure all of this will stop."

He looked up. "But can it really be true. Can we trust any of it?"

"There's one more way to find out and convince you of the reality," beamed Sarah. "Maps of the parish."

Half an hour later, they had it. The proof. John G. Taylor's house had once stood in the grounds of what was now a hospital. Taylor's name was even scratched inside the little drawing of the house. Sarah gave Jamie a quizzical look and he responded, at last, with a smile.

* * *

Jamie's mum flicked through the various pages once again, mouth screwed up, digesting all the facts over and over. Sitting across the kitchen table from her, Jamie and Sarah waited.

At last, Jamie couldn't contain his impatience any longer. "Well? What do you think, Mum?"

Mum looked at him. "It's all very strange." She thought again for a moment. Jamie sighed in exasperation. "What you're saying, Jamie, is that all of this is linked to the dream you've had?"

"Not just *one* dream, lots of dreams. Tim's had them, too. Nightmares, about the man called Rooster, and later, the pawnbroker. Then the stuff about the houses. "

"But you couldn't find anything about the big house, the one where you and Tim first went to?"

Jamie shook his head sadly. "Nothing to go on. But the house where the Taylors lived, it's there!"

Mum looked at the photocopied papers again. "I can see. You've got the whole history of the street, here. *Our* street. All the names, businesses, houses, even the little school that used to be at the top. You must have learnt how to do all this stuff at your own school."

"We did," said Sarah. "We learned about the first census in 1801, how they developed into a nationwide survey in 1861, then how every ten years one was to be taken of the entire country. The street directories…"

Jamie broke in, "Yeah, we learned all *that,* but we didn't learn anything about this!" His finger jabbed at the papers. "All of this has come from my dreams. The details, the faces, what the house looked like. What we've got to do is go up to where Mr Taylor's house stood and see if it's the same."

"It won't be the same," laughed Mum. "It's an old hospital now, and most of it is empty buildings. They'll be pulling it down soon to make way for more houses, probably."

"All the more reason why we should go there."

He looked at Sarah and she nodded. His mum shrugged and sat back in her chair. "It seems like you two detectives have made up your minds." She went to the window and looked out across the lawn. "It's just…" She turned around and her eyes were steady and a little stern, "Jamie, don't get angry, but you have a very *vivid* imagination. What if all of the stuff you've learned in school, is what's triggered off all of this in your mind?"

Before Jamie could raise his voice in protest, Sarah gently laid her hand on his arm. It was enough and he slowly relaxed. "No, Mum," he replied, calmly, "it's the other way round. My dreams came first, *then* we discovered the truth."

Mum nodded, reluctant to press her son still further. "All right, I hear what you're saying, but couldn't it have been the house? Where you fell asleep and…" She noted their looks. Her shoulders drooped. "Well, the hospital's only up the road, but I want you both to be careful, you hear? And if the police catch you..." Her voice trailed away.

"We'll be careful," said Sarah and looked at Jamie who gave a confident nod.

His mother seemed satisfied.

What Jamie had omitted to say was that they'd also discovered the name of a pawnbroker's business in Hamilton Square and it was Jamie's intention to go there first.

* * *

It was raining as they stood amongst the debris of what had once been the pawnbroker's shop. Not so long ago, other businesses had thrived here but now the area was condemned and soon everything would be cleared to make way for new housing.

"If we're going to find anything here," said Jamie, pulling up his collar, "we're going to have to work fast. Time is definitely working against us."

He hadn't dressed for rain and his thin t-shirt was soon soaked through. As he started picking his way through the broken stones and bits of timber, he looked across at Sarah who was sheltering in a crumbling doorway. She watched him with something like admiration. On the way over, she'd told him he was unlike any of the other boys at school. He was not silly and interested in only sweets and football. He could actually make conversation, which was a rare thing for a boy of *any* age. She smiled at him and he felt the heat rising from under his damp collar. He pressed on.

Treading carefully amongst the fallen masonry, he stopped and looked about him. There was nothing here. No sign of any sort of business. It was all just another ruin, a heap of dead stones. "It's hopeless," he said, walking back to her. "We'll never find anything."

He stood beside her in the doorway and looked up at the leaden sky. "It was stupid of me to come here. A total waste of time."

She pressed her hand on his shoulder. "No, it wasn't. We have to try and follow every lead, no matter how silly it may seem. Let's go to the hospital now and see what we can find there."

He looked at her. What she said made complete sense, but he still believed that there was something here. A feeling had brought him to this place, a tiny glimmer of hope, echoed in his dream.

"I know this is the place. When I came here before, the entrance ..." he kicked at the debris close by, "was just here, but now, it all seems so different. Can you remember what we saw on the plans?"

She frowned. "I'm not sure. It all looks such a mess, nothing like the plans."

"In the dream, the one where they first met him to try their luck with the jewellery, they came in through here." He stepped out into the rain again, closing his eyes to conjure up the images. "They went to more than one shop but it was *this* one, *this* pawnbroker, who decided to follow them and to get his greedy hands on what he knew was a fortune."

He stepped across to the far wall and pressed his hands flat against it. The bricks were black with age, the mortar damp and loose. "At the back of the shop would be his living area, so there must be..." Keeping his eyes closed, he carefully traced a path with his hands across the flaking surface of the bricks. Then he stopped and his eyes sprang open. He could see it, as clearly as if it was still there. "It's here."

Sarah came over to him, touching the bricks for herself, engrossed, the rain forgotten. "I can't feel anything," she said softly.

Jamie took a step back and gazed at the wall with a new intensity. Gradually, the smile spread across his face. "I can see it," he said at last. "I can see it as plain as day – can't you?"

She shook her head. "I want to, Jamie, I really do, but all I see is just bricks, looking all the same, black and featureless, with the mortar…" Frowning deeply, she turned to him, eyes wide with excitement. "Jamie," she gasped, "I can see it! This area," she made a flourish with her hand, "look at the mortar – it's more recent."

He wanting to jump and down with joy. "It's a bricked-up entrance, Sarah. The entrance to his home!"

She stood and stared. "How do we get inside? We haven't got anything to knock it through with."

He gave a wink. "There is a way. You go and check that there's nobody about, just in case."

By now, the rain was hammering down and when she went and took a glance down the old alleyway that once led to the buildings, she saw no one. Behind her, Jamie was becoming increasingly excited. She smiled and called, "There's no one about. What are we going to do?"

He nodded, took a few steps backwards, closed his eyes and took a deep breath.

Sarah screamed as he charged forward, hitting the old bricks with a sickening thud, his shoulder jarring against the roughened surface. He cried out and bent double, his right hand clutching at his left bicep. "It's solid," he hissed as she stepped up to him, concern etched into her face. "I'm all right." He gritted his teeth and prepared to take another step back.

Suddenly, as if some unseen hand of immense strength had got to work, the wall groaned and, slowly at first, bricks fell one by one. Clouds of dust and ancient chunks of clay splattered and spluttered as the entire edifice swayed, as if experiencing a minor earthquake.

"What's happening?" shouted Sarah above the rain – rain which seemed to be growing louder by the second. Looking at her through the veil of hair plastered to his face, Jamie shrugged and decided to help the demolition work on its way. He snapped his foot against the wall, kicking it with all his strength. A great blast drowned even the sound of the rain for a moment, as the bricks completely gave way to reveal a gaping hole.

"It's the entrance!" Jamie yelled. "It has to be – the old entrance to the back of the pawnbroker's shop where he lived."

"It's unbelievable," Sarah said. "How can it have remained here, hidden away for so many years?"

Jamie had no answer and only one thought – to go inside.

He stepped through the hole, with Sarah close behind. They both stopped.

The rain was nothing more than a series of distant thuds now. Above them, the roof remained intact, giving them complete shelter from the elements. Slowly, their eyes grew accustomed to the gloom, but the furthest corners were still consumed by the blackness. He pulled out his mobile, tried the torch. "It's like in the house," he said, defeated. "There's no signal. Worse than that, nothing works." Like a blind person, Jamie stretched out his hands in front of him and groped forward into the unknown. Behind him, Sarah's ragged, uneven breathing told him she was afraid. He wished he could turn to her and tell her that it was all a mistake – that they should run away and find a fast-food restaurant and forget all about this whole miserable business. But he couldn't. Something mysterious and powerful was compelling him to press on, so he kept moving forward, infinitely slowly, desperate to stumble across something, *anything*, that would justify this ludicrous adventure.

"Jamie," came Sarah's voice, low and strained. "Jamie… there's someone in here…"

He stopped, not certain whether to flee, or continue. He listened but heard nothing. Turning to reach out and find her in the total blackness, he gently called her name. She loomed before him, nothing but a smudge in the darkness. And then she tripped, yelped and fell into his arms.

He held her, feeling her in his embrace, her heart slamming against him, her breath blowing into his neck. "It's all right," he whispered. Straining to pick out any sounds or movements that might reveal what lurked in the room, Jamie squinted over Sarah's shoulder and managed to make out what could have been an old filing cabinet, a broken table, two or three chairs. They were all lying shattered about the ground, and papers were strewn everywhere. Squinting, he wondered why the hole in the wall didn't cast more light on everything.

And then he saw the reason and a new, much stronger terror gripped him.

Something huge filled the hole, blocking out the light. Whatever it was, it pulsed with wickedness, a perverse, palpable feeling of menace emanating from its centre. Jamie's limbs turned to liquid, the strength leaking from him, almost as if the presence itself had drained him of all his resolve. He desperately wanted to sleep, to fall down, curl up and slide into unconsciousness.

Hands were shaking him violently and he snapped his head up, suddenly wide awake. Sarah's face pressed in close to his. "Jamie," she was saying, "we've got to get out of here – now!"

She was pulling him and he allowed her to take him towards the gap in the wall. And the shape.

They both broke into a run, arms thrashing towards the dark presence, screaming in unison, the adrenalin coursing through their bodies giving them the strength and the determination to find their way out.

And then, all at once, they were tumbling out into the daylight and the pelting rain, rolling over into the dirt, not stopping to wait and check that the shape, or whatever it was, had gone. Scrambling to their feet, they ran at top speed down the alleyway. They ran on until they reached the shopping precinct, with loud traffic and streams of people passing by, the stores offering them the chance for safety, for sanctuary.

Sheltering under the large entrance of a department store, they clung onto one another, taking in great gulps of air, trying to regain some of their composure.

"What *was* that?" gasped Jamie at last, the presence of so many shoppers, the normality of everyday life, giving him the courage to face the impossibility and the stark, naked horror of what they'd experienced.

"I don't know," answered Sarah, wringing her hands as her wide, frightened eyes scanned the crowds as if she expected to see the terrible presence striding towards them. "Whatever it was, it scared the hell out of me!" She shook her head. "It was so huge and menacing and... and ..."

"Evil." Jamie's word hung in the air, as he cast his mind back to the remains of the pawnbroker's shop and what they'd found there. The reason for everything. The dreams, the murders... He held her tight. "Come on," he said, "let's get ourselves a burger and think about what all of this means."

They sat across from each other, staring into their plates of food, the warmth of the interior drying their sodden clothes. Beyond the window, the rain had petered out into a drizzle. Life went on in its usual, mundane way. Shoppers, overladen with bags; parents with howling children, teenagers laughing raucously. All oblivious to the trauma that consumed both Jamie and Sarah, making them confused and afraid.

"Jamie." Her voice cut through his thoughts and he looked into her bright, beautiful eyes. "We have to go back."

He almost choked. "What? You've got to be joking!"

She was adamant. "No, we've got to, Jamie. There's something in there, and not just that... that *presence*. A clue, a name, something. We'll go back to yours, get a torch and then have a proper look."

"And that... *thing*. What about that?"

She shrugged. "I don't think it was anything dangerous."

"*What?* You saw it, it was *real*, Sarah!"

"It *seemed* real, but we were frightened and the dark plays tricks. It could have been a shadow... anything."

"You don't believe that. You know as well as I do that it was something. Something evil."

"I did at first, yes, but now thinking about it... how could it be real?" Shaking her head, she dropped her eyes to the remnants of her burger and pushed it around with her plastic fork. "We went there to find evidence of the pawnbroker, so we were already in a heightened state of... suggestion."

"Suggestion? Like hypnotists use, you mean? You think that's it? Honestly?"

"If it was real, how come we just ran through it?"

He looked around the dining area, his eyes sweeping over the people and their faces. Happy, thoughtful, sad. None seemed afraid. But fear was what his face showed, he felt sure. "I know it was real. You don't just think up things like that. You know it, too." He looked at her. "You're just too afraid to admit it."

Sarah reached out her hand and very gently laid it over his. "Jamie... Maybe you're right, I don't know, but what I do know is we must find out what all of this means. Your dreams led us to that place. What we found in the library confirmed everything. But why do you keep having those dreams? Are they a message, a cry for help... what?"

"I don't know, Sarah." His voice was flat, defeated. She squeezed his hand and, after a moment, he stood up. "I suppose you're right. We may have to go back. There is something there, some answers. Now we know what to expect, we can..." He shrugged, doing his utmost to sound brave, but inside he was falling apart. "But before we do anything, we're going to the house."

"The house?"

"Taylor's house," he explained, "the hospital. The answers might be there, which means we may not even have to go back to that other place. If we can find a clue or something at the hospital, perhaps we can bring all of this to an end."

Before she could either agree or disagree, he was striding towards the exit. He stopped and looked skywards. The rain had stopped, strands of blue showing through the blanket of clouds. Behind him, he felt Sarah moving up close. "It's going to be a nice day," she said. He looked at her and sighed.

* * *

No one stopped them as they walked up the broad hospital approach road. They passed a few low-level buildings which still served the local community for things such as minor accidents and anti-natal clinics, and carried on to the old maternity hospital. An imposing building, it stood silent and empty, awaiting whatever fate had been determined for it by the local government. Jamie stopped and blew out a loud breath.

"This isn't it."

Sarah sucked in her lips. "Of course not, silly. This is the hospital that was built on the site of your house."

"Taylor's house," Jamie corrected her.

Sensing his mood, she squeezed his hand. "Let's look around the back."

He followed her to the side of the building and from there, they edged their way to the far corner. Here, they stopped and looked out across a large, open square of grass. Something stirred in Jamie's mind. It looked strangely familiar, despite having changed so much. Screwing up his eyes, he gestured to something in the far corner of the field. "What's that over there?

Sarah followed his pointing finger. "It's a pond, I think." She went to move towards it but Jamie grabbed her by the arm. She glared at him and pulled herself free. "What's the matter?"

"Don't go over there," he said, voice scarcely above a whisper. "Please, just stay here with me."

"It's nothing but a pond, Jamie. There's no demons or hobgoblins there."

His eyes never left hers. "In that pond, Josh..." He closed his eyes, recalling the stark image of his dream. "He died in there." He slapped his hands against his face, the images returning in a rush and he whimpered, staggering backwards. Josh, the blood pumping from his wound, pitching into the water... the water turning bright red.

Sarah gently pulled his hands from his face and he gazed into her soft, smiling face. "Even if that's true, which I'm sure it is," she said soothingly, "it all happened a long, long time ago. There won't be anything there now." She gave him another brave smile and, before he could say anything more, she marched resolutely across the lawn to the scene of Josh's murder.

He watched her striding off, not daring to move himself. He saw her stand next to the water for a moment before bending down and dipping her hand in. She looked back at him and shook her head. She returned, the water still dripping from her fingertips, a look of disappointment on her face. "Nothing, nothing at all except for pondweed. Let's go back to the pawnbroker's. Maybe we could..."

"No." Jamie swallowed hard. "No, that has to be it. It used to be a fountain. Long ago. When Taylor lived here, all of this was a garden." He swung around to stare at the hospital. "There," he pointed towards an old green door, "that was where the porch doors opened. Through them, Taylor could keep his eyes on Bert and Annabel as they played. It's all here. Or at least it was. And that pond," he turned again and punched his fist into his hand, "it's the site of the fountain! It's where Josh fell after being stabbed. And Tim, he would have known it, too, because he had the same dream. He would have come here, to see for himself. To prove to himself that it was all true, that it all happened!"

His hands shot towards her and he took her by the arms, shaking her. "Sarah… he's here! Tim!" He ran off, back to the front of the building.

Sarah stood, mouth gaping, not sure what to make of any of it. As she watched him rush away, she experienced an inexplicable desire to turn away, causing her to stop. She looked again at the pond. A shape lingered there. Was it yet another shadow, this time caused by the overhanging tree branches, or was it something else? She thought she saw, standing at the water's edge, a figure wearing a large, broad-brimmed hat. She squeezed her eyes shut for a moment and reopened them. There was nothing; the only sight the pond, the only sound the breeze rustling through the leaves. Whoever it was had gone. It was just her mind playing tricks, sent into overdrive by the events of the day.

Cursing herself for being so silly, she ran off after Jamie. She found him rooted to the spot, a wild, haunted look in his eyes. "Jamie?"

Ignoring her, he strode towards the entrance. She called after him, but he wasn't stopping for anybody. Exasperated, she followed.

He stood reading the large metal plaque next to the double doors and, without waiting, pushed the door open and stepped inside.

"Jamie!"

Sarah raced up to the door and stopped.

Jamie was frozen, looking at her, eyes round and wet. A single tear rolled down his cheek. He glanced to his left and she followed his gaze.

Propped up against the inside wall was Tim's bike.

Gathering

Past and future.

A heady mix, one which created confusion, anxiety, impatience. Anger and hate.

They all combined to harden the pawnbroker's heart, cloud his judgement, consuming him with desire. And malice towards those who possessed what he, too, longed to possess.

But now the waiting was almost over and he felt intoxicated at the prospect of holding what was his once more. Avarice had eaten away at him, twisted him into a perverse and distorted thing. A vessel containing the capacity for extreme violence.

Years, the past, all had blurred. The powers he had gained had delivered him to this juncture, his patience and determination rewarded at last. Now, nothing could divert him from his path.

He recited once more the ancient texts that had brought him to this place. A place of darkness, of possession. And the creature that had enabled him to pass between the distant shores of time had taken his soul as its payment. A small price to pay. Or so the pawnbroker believed.

What he did not know, had not even questioned, was the origin of the creature; its domain, the place where it was spawned. If he had, perhaps he might have paused and considered the consequence of his endeavours. For the creature was from the realm of evil that lurks beyond the physical world, a place of immeasurable torment, of the most extreme excesses, a place in which its inhabitants revel in the pain and suffering of others. Humankind.

The creature cared nothing for the pawnbroker's grasping greed. All it cared for was the gathering of souls, souls of the lost, to feed its malevolence, and the pawnbroker's was just one more to add to its growing tally. A tally that stretched down through the ages, to the very dawn of mankind itself.

Having done many things that would have condemned any man to hell, the pawnbroker no longer had any control over his actions. He could not stop, not now that the goal was within his grasp. The jewels. His machinations had brought him within sight of a victory he felt was deservedly his. Riches beyond measure. An opportunity to find a kind of peace.

There was no going back. That much he knew. If the taking of one more life would bring him what he desired, then so be it. What difference would one more make? Or two? Or a dozen? Nothing was going to bar him from his victory.

He'd watched and he'd waited.

He'd witnessed their pitiful attempts, scoffed at their infantile research. Even though they had come so close to finding him, of learning something about his life, he dismissed their efforts as foolish and futile. What did any of it matter? Everything was spiralling towards the only conceivable outcome – his seizure of the jewels. After so long, after so much suffering, pain and anguish, they were so tantalisingly close he could almost taste them.

But, consumed as he was by his own greed, he never stopped to consider that fate might still play a part – that these insignificant fools, as he often thought them to be, might still thwart him. He underestimated them and that was the chink in his otherwise impenetrable armour of self-assuredness. He was blind to their determination.

And their friendship. Their love.

Having lived a solitary life, he did not value the strength or power that being loved can give. He dismissed it as nonsense. And there was his undoing.

The creature knew this. But it did not care.

It only cared to feed its own desire.

The desire for souls.

Blind to any doubts, putting aside any misgivings, the pawnbroker prepared himself for the final act. He accepted that more lives would have to be shed, but they would be a price worth paying. And now, of course, he had an acolyte. His key to success. Long ago, it had been Josh. Now, it was another who would help him. In the murky half-light between past and present, he wandered and waited, assured that the final act would be played out soon.

And so it was.

Chapter Twenty

Another Meeting, Another Time

With the discovery of Tim's bike, they both knew what to do. Without any hesitation, they returned to Jamie's house, little more than ten minutes away and grabbed a couple of torches. Jamie led Sarah to the backyard and the small shed where he kept his bikes.

"This is my new one," he said, pulling out a fine-looking mountain bike, its tyres barely worn. It was in stark contrast to the rusted heap behind it, its own tyres so thin they were in danger of splitting at any moment. "You take the new one," he said.

This was not a time to argue, so she sat astride it and waited for Jamie to find some oil and squirt it into the chain of the older bicycle. Then, all set, they rode off, pedalling as if their lives depended on it, towards the pawnbroker's shop.

At the entrance, they stopped outside the gaping hole in the brickwork and looked at each other. "Are we doing the right thing?" he asked her.

Sarah dismounted and leaned the mountain bike against the adjacent wall. "You know we are," she said, with a tight smile.

Grunting, he threw his own bike to the ground, pulled out the torch and switched it on. "Stay close," he said and stepped inside.

Daylight immediately retreated.

They were once more in the realm of permanent night. Even so, the interior was darker than he remembered, but the torch gave some comfort, its strong beam cutting through the gloom. Able to pick out the details with far greater ease than last time, he went straight to the filing cabinet. He gestured to Sarah to follow.

But Sarah wasn't moving. She stood rigid, gazing at something. He stepped up to her, shaking her arm. "Sarah," he hissed, "what is it?"

Without a word, he followed her gaze, training the torchlight into the corner. There was a desk, piled high with papers and ledgers. Beyond, behind the desk, huddled over one such ledger, sat a shape. Ominous and solid-looking, the only discernible movement being the rise and fall of its shoulders as it breathed. It was a man, right hand clutching a pencil, scrawling it across the open book. Beside him was a broad-brimmed hat.

The pawnbroker!

Time stood still, oppressive silence descending heavily like a huge, dead weight. Everything, even the slightest intake of breath, became amplified to deafening proportions.

Rooted to the spot, Jamie slowly lowered the torch and turned his incredulous face towards Sarah. Her eyes, so wide and full of terror, shone like beacons, so brightly Jamie felt sure they would alert the pawnbroker to their presence.

If, of course, he was real.

This thought snapped Jamie out of his trance. For one insane moment, he believed he might burst out laughing. Of course he wasn't real, at least not in *this* world. What they both saw was a memory, frozen in time, like a paused frame on a celluloid film – an image from times past.

Feeling detached from what he saw, viewing things from a distance, he took a step, reached out his hand and touched figure's shoulder. He heard Sarah gasp.

Nothing happened. There was no substance to the figure, no solidity. It continued writing, unaware of Jamie's presence. Mesmerised by the claw-like hand, Jamie peered closer, following the words as they appeared on the page.

I am virtually there. The waiting is nearly at an end. I have the treasure within my grasp… thanks… to…

Holding his breath, Jamie waited for the pawnbroker to scribble down the last word, a word he already knew and, had he been able to, could have written himself.

Instead, with its hand poised above the page, the figure stopped and turned its head.

The pawnbroker's face stared back, a face of stretched, dried parchment, grey, ashen and sunken. Its eyes were black, lifeless coals, its thin, bluish mouth filled with chipped and broken teeth, and the stench exuding from that rotting hole was sharp and acidic, laced with the tang of vomit and rancid with decay. Clamping his hand to his mouth and nose, Jamie groaned and staggered backwards.

Its voice rattled like the sound of nails in a rusty can. "Jamie," it said, and its white, wormy fingers squeezed the pencil with such intensity it snapped in two.

Jamie screamed but could not move. Overwhelming terror gripped him. His mind reeled, his senses in chaos. He stood transfixed as the figure rose to its full height, the black mouth gaping open, those hands reaching out to grip him around the throat, extinguish his life. "Jamie, my lovely…"

A hand grabbed him by the collar, yanking him back with surprising force, pulling him away from the loathsome figure which, impossibly, set off a loud, insane-sounding cackling.

Sarah held Jamie tightly in her arms. He looked towards the table. All thoughts of images on film and memories frozen in time disappeared. This was no spectre or ghost, no phantom from a long dead world; this was a real, physical thing, with evil intent in its every move. Even as he stood and stared, he saw it reach inside its coat to produce a wickedly glinting blade, one Jamie knew well. He'd seen it in his dreams and he knew what it could do.

They both screamed, voices shrill and at breaking point. In a blur, they whirled away, Sarah taking the lead, scrambling over the broken, littered floor towards the entrance, frantic, desperate to escape. Trembling hands trained the torches to pick out the gap. Beyond, the daylight waited like a warm, welcoming friend and they stumbled out into the cool afternoon, scooped up their bikes and raced, heads down, from that ghastly, unearthly place.

They did not stop until they cascaded into Jamie's backyard. He bolted the door and turned to look into Sarah's eyes. And then they embraced.

Chapter Twenty-One

Respite… or Worse?

The park was quiet, less busy than usual, the wet weather keeping almost everyone away. They both sat in silence, the image of the pawnbroker consuming them with terror. Neither felt able to speak, both lost in their thoughts.

As the silence continued, Jamie's unease grew until he could suffer it no longer. He stood up, throwing his head back to glare at the grey sky. "What are we going to do, Sarah?"

He swung around and looked at her. Head down, hair hanging like curtains to hide her face, her voice trembled as she muttered, "I don't know."

"We have to do something. Tell someone. Not just Mum – I mean someone important. This is real – what we experienced was *real.*"

"I know," she said, without moving. "I never believed such a thing could be possible." She looked up at him, tears trailing down her cheeks, eyes red and puffy. "Maybe the police?"

He dismissed the suggestion instantly, swatting the words away with the wave of a hand. "They'd laugh at us – probably have us for wasting their precious time."

She shrugged, totally at a loss. "I can't think who we can tell, if not…" Suddenly, it was as if a light went on in her face and she grinned. "I know – *Mr Morris*! He'll know what to do."

"*Morris*? You've got to be joking, Sarah – he'll probably report us to the Head, inform our parents or something."

"No, he won't do any of that, Jamie. Mr Morris *loves* history – he'll be able to tell us anything we don't already know and…" She stopped at his look and curbed her excitement. "We have to try," she said firmly.

"It's stupid. He's on holiday, like us. We can't just go banging on his door and telling him, 'Ooh, ooh, Mr Morris, sir, we found a ghost and he's come back to murder us!' He'll burst out laughing and slam the door in our face."

"He wouldn't."

"Of course he would – wouldn't you? Imagine, somebody coming up to you and telling you such a cock-and-bull story. You wouldn't believe it, would you?"

She went to speak, but when she opened her mouth, no words came out. Instead, shoulders drooping, she went back to staring at the ground. "He might know what to do, that's all. If I talked to him, convinced him, he might just… I don't know. He likes me. We get on. He'd help, I know he would."

"How would he help? By marching us to our parents and telling them that we've broken into *two* buildings? Sarah, we could end up in court!"

"Don't be silly. We haven't done anything wrong."

"I'd say breaking and entering is pretty wrong, wouldn't you?"

"But he'll be able to advise us what to do."

"About a ghost from the past? Sarah, he'll think we're mad." He sat again, wringing his hands. "Everyone will think we're mad."

They walked aimlessly around the park for a long time, pushing their bikes as they went, thoroughly soaked through by now but not caring at all about the rain. Their only thoughts were of the pawnbroker and the look on his awful, nightmarish face.

Stopping by the lake, they propped their bikes against the railings and stared at the ducks swimming by.

"Wish I was a duck," muttered Jamie, despair thick in his voice.

"Do you? Me too."

"I wish… I wish I'd never set foot inside that house. If I'd been stronger, I would have stood up to Tim, told him no. But I couldn't… He's my only friend. If I'd refused to do what he asked, I might have lost him. Then I'd be alone."

He gave a start as her hand folded over his. "No, you wouldn't."

The look in her eyes caused the strength to leak from his limbs and he held onto the railings, wanting to grin, wanting to cry out and tell her, tell the whole world, how he felt towards her. Instead, he simply smiled.

Sarah smiled too.

But only for a moment.

Something caught her eye and all at once everything changed. Her hand flew to her mouth, suppressing a scream. For one awful moment, Jamie thought the pawnbroker had appeared again. But when he swung round to follow her gaze, he saw it wasn't the fiend, but something almost as frightening. Strolling along the far side of the lake was a tall man, wearing a top hat, who held two children by the hand. A girl and a boy.

Blinking, attempting to dispel the vision, Jamie stood frozen, gazing upon a flickering scene from an old film, images impressed upon the fabric of space. There could be no other explanation. It was Bert, Annabel and Mr Taylor, out for an afternoon walk.

As they came closer, their features grew more distinct. They were exactly as they appeared in his dreams. He felt Sarah's hand gripping his and he shot her a glance, saw the incredulity there, and said, "It's them."

"How…?"

Shaking his head, Jamie turned to them again and watched them throwing bread to the ducks. An ordinary, everyday scene, a glimpse into the past. But in Bert's world, it wasn't raining. Somehow, he and Sarah had been given the privilege of viewing the same moment, but in another time, another dimension. "I've read somewhere, or seen something about this. How time-travel is a possibility due to the existence of multiple, parallel universes. They've actually discovered that –"

He turned to explain the rest of this theory, but she wasn't there. She was charging towards the three figures from an age gone by. They, however, appeared oblivious to her approach and continued throwing their bread, laughing loudly as the ducks squabbled and fought for the scraps.

"Sarah!" Jamie shouted, something warning him they shouldn't interfere. "Sarah, don't get too close."

She stopped, breathless but elated and threw out her arms in a question: "What?"

At that instant, the three figures also stopped and turned their faces turned towards Jamie. For a moment, their eyes locked. With deliberate slowness, Mr Taylor raised his hand in a gesture of greeting. Beside him, the two youngsters joined in, grinning. Soon, they were waving their hands in frantic, uncontained joy.

He didn't know what any of this meant. Regardless of their obvious happiness, Jamie experienced a growing sense of unease. He stepped away from the railings and his bike, as if moved by invisible fingers, suddenly crashed to the ground. Stunned, he bent to pick it up and when he straightened again and looked, they had gone. Simply vanished.

Approaching the area where they had stood, Sarah let out a long wail of utter despair. She fell to her knees, face buried in her hands. Forgetting his bike, Jamie tore around the lake to her side. He got down on the wet ground and, the pounding rain forgotten, put his arms around her and she fell against his chest, great sobs racking her slender frame.

Gradually, the rain eased. A strange, eerie quiet descended upon the park. Not even a bird was singing. Only the ducks, as they swam across the water, made any sort of noise.

The ducks!

Turning to the water, Jamie and Sarah watched with wide, disbelieving eyes as the ducks squabbled and fought for the last few scraps of bread which still floated on the surface of the lake. Bread that had been thrown to them more than a hundred years ago.

* * *

That night, Jamie had the strangest dream of all. Instead of the usual catalogue of terrible, terrifying events, he was treated to a series of quiet scenes in which Mr and Mrs Taylor, together with Bert and Annabel, spent joyful moments picnicking in sun-lit fields, their laughter mingling with the birdsong and the happiness of it all so complete that Jamie felt he could actually touch it.

He awoke refreshed and, for the first time for days, relaxed, filled with new sense of confidence. Downstairs, Mum was singing to herself and it was as if a new page had been turned. Jamie allowed himself to believe the worst was over; that perhaps his meeting with the pawnbroker had in some way broken the spell under which they had all been since his first visit to the Big House.

Mum smiled broadly as she slid two slices of buttered toast onto his plate. He raised a quizzical eyebrow. "Why are you so happy?"

She pursed her lips. "Dad rang."

Jamie's heart leapt but he didn't say anything. He'd been disappointed too often in the past, his hopes that Dad might come home dashed as yet another row between his parents had sabotaged any plans.

"I told him some more about what you've been going through." She paused, but if she was expecting an outburst, Jamie didn't give her one. He simply looked and waited. Sufficiently emboldened, she continued, "He's very concerned, Jamie. But he understands and... well, he wants to come and see us. I said he could."

Jamie bit down on his toast. Inside, his stomach was doing somersaults. He hadn't seen his Dad for so long...

The telephone trilled into life. As Mum lifted up the receiver, Jamie strained to hear who the caller might be. Tim's mum called often now, desperate for any information about her son. "Still nothing," said Jamie's mum. She came back and stood, shaking her head. "It's all so sad," was all she said, but Jamie knew exactly what she meant.

Later, in his room, Jamie answered another e-mail from Sarah. Despite his misgivings, she'd gone ahead and spoken with Mr Morris. Any anger he felt soon faded. After all, it was Sarah, and he could forgive Sarah anything. So he wrote back, *OK, if you think it will help.* They arranged to meet Mr Morris that afternoon and, as Jamie pulled on his jeans, he wondered if anything good would come out of it. Even if it did, the thought of meeting a teacher in the holidays made Jamie cringe.

* * *

Away from the classroom, Mr Morris seemed a nice enough man. He probably always was, thought Jamie as he sat on the sofa. He'd listened to Jamie's story with interest, even going so far as to take notes in a little battered book. When the story was brought up-to-date, Morris took a moment to read over what he had written before sitting in his armchair, measuring Jamie with a long, hard look.

"That's one hell of a story," he said.

Jamie bristled, but before he could reply, Sarah, perhaps anticipating what was about to happen, jumped in, her voice light and even. "Mr Morris, you don't seriously think we're making any of this up?"

Morris held up his hand, "No, don't get me wrong. Neither of you." He smiled. "I watched the local news, the story about Tim's disappearance. Nobody has a clue what's going on, so I know for sure none of this is in your imagination. Tell you what, let's go and take a look at this old pawnbroker shop."

Jamie gaped and sat up. "What?"

Laughing now, Morris stood up, collecting his car keys from the table under the window. "Nothing like a bit of primary evidence to get the juices flowing."

* * *

Less than ten minutes later, Morris emerged from the wreckage. He appeared a lot more serious than before and considered the other two with a dark look. "There's something…"

"You mean, you could *feel* it," said Jamie, breathlessly. He held onto Sarah's arm. This could be the confirmation they both needed – the proof none of this was in their heads!

"It could be the age of the place, the old bricks, the bits of furniture…" Morris shook his head. "I don't know. But… it's weird, let's put it that way." He turned to take another look at the remains. "It's incredible that you found this place. I never would have believed… I mean, it must be well over a hundred and fifty years old. Perhaps more. To think they're going to wipe all of this clean off the map, as if it never existed, to make way for houses, for God's sake."

Shaking his head, he stepped up close to them. "When Sarah first told me about this, I began some research of my own. You see, Jamie," he leaned forward, "I have made a particular study of crime and punishment in Victorian Liverpool – and that includes Birkenhead." He dipped inside his jacket and brought out a book. He read from his notes. "A pawnbroker... I've discovered details of the murders, the arrests. It was a *cause célèbre* at the time."

"A what?"

"A big story – headline news. This pawnbroker of yours terrorised this area, using intimidation and violence to gather his ill-gotten gains. He was caught, convicted and..." his smile broadened, "... sentenced."

Together, they ambled along the alleyway to the main road. Across the street stood Morris's car. "I'm going to look into this further," he said. "Whatever you've unearthed, it's extremely interesting."

"And what about the other bits?" Jamie sensed Sarah tensing next to him. He took her hand, squeezed it, ignoring Morris' surprised look. "The house? The jewels? Bert and Annabel? It's all linked. The pawnbroker, he wants the jewels." He pulled in a breath. "He *still* wants them."

The silence stretched out. Morris scanned his book again, probably for something to do.

"You don't believe it."

His head came up. "I believe you've uncovered the maniac's hideout. I believe that, somehow, you've discovered the details of his foulest crimes. Anything more, well, we'll have to wait and see."

Morris wore his cloak of deception well, a lifetime of pretending to be angry with children in the classroom having honed his acting skills to a high level. He was acting now, Jamie knew it. "Like I say, you don't believe it. You pretend you do, but deep down..."

"You did say you felt something in there," interjected Sarah quickly. "You have to accept that, Mr Morris."

"Yes, well... Like I said, it's old. Old houses, buildings, they have... an *atmosphere*. Look, Sarah, I'm not a paranormal investigator. I'm a history teacher. I'm interested in facts, not ghosts. Maybe there is something there, some energy from a tortured soul, but…" He smiled. Tried to make it warm. "I'll go home, do some more research. You never know, I might be able to match whatever I find with your dreams, Jamie. I'll do my best."

"Thanks anyway," said Jamie.

* * *

Morris took his leave and crossed over to his waiting car. As he put the key in the door, he turned and smiled at the two of them, their affection for each other so obvious. Nice kids, he thought. Jamie rarely sparked in class, but here he seemed in his element somehow. A bright, cheerful lad. Not unlike Jake used to be.

Sighing, he opened the car door and promised himself to give his son a ring as soon he got home.

A sideways glance would have revealed something more. A figure, dark and indistinct, stood in a doorway, silently watching the teacher. Something glinted in his hand and he was already crossing the road before Morris had even turned on the ignition.

Chapter Twenty-Two

All Things Come to Pass…

Together, they stood on the threshold of the old house. Having cycled there at a furious pace, both now sagged over the handlebars of their bikes, panting. For Jamie, this was the culmination of weeks of confusion and fear. He knew if he was to bring it all to an end, he must once again step inside.

Three hours previously, Jamie had slid out of bed, gripped with a curious elation. No dreams had interrupted his sleep and, seeming to underline this new-found positivity, when he threw back his bedroom curtains the sunshine streamed in. Closing his eyes, he sighed deeply and let the warmth fill him with its golden glow.

Everything changed when he went downstairs.

He'd found his mother sitting at the table, a cold cup of coffee clasped in her hands, staring at the wall with empty eyes. She didn't flinch when he sat down opposite her. "Mum?"

She looked at him and shook her head. "Oh Jamie, it's just too awful. It was on the news, first thing. Dreadful."

"What was? What's happened?" Surely nothing had happened to his dad? Jamie's heart started to thump uncomfortably.

Reaching out to stroke his cheek, his mother continued, in a hushed tone that was almost reverent, "I've known him for years, since school. He was… such a *nice* man. Then, when he got a job at your school, well, it was just like… Oh God!" She dropped her head, coffee forgotten, and squeezed a finger and thumb into her eyes. "I was good friends with his wife, you see, and when she passed away, I became…"

"Mum, who are you talking about?"

Though her eyes were swimming with tears, she managed to focus on his face. "Your history teacher, Mr Morris. He's dead. Murdered."

* * *

"I can't believe it," said Sarah down the phone. "We were only with him yesterday."

"I know. Have you seen the reports? They're all over the internet. Kids have started posting things on Facebook, not all of it all very complimentary."

"Yeah… yeah, I'm looking now… God, Jamie, this is…"

The silence hung between them and he allowed her time to take in the enormity of what she was reading. "Jamie, have you read this? Yes, of course you have. I mean… the *way* he was killed? The knife thrust to his throat, it's exactly like what happened to –"

"Rooster. I know." He dragged in a breath. "It was him."

There was no need to elaborate. The killing of Mr Morris bore all the trademarks of the pawnbroker. A single cut into the throat, delivered with incredible ferocity and power. The police were baffled. A seemingly unprovoked attack, for no purpose or reason, had ended the life of a deeply respected and immensely popular teacher. Both on radio and local television, the head teacher gushed with praise for his late colleague, going into great detail about how he'd helped so many, how much he'd be missed, and how he had even given up his own time during the holidays to help some students with their studies.

Jamie winced at that. If he and Sarah hadn't involved him in their research, he'd still be alive, enjoying his holiday, looking forward to –

His e-mail pinged, bringing him out of his morbid daydreaming. Hastily, he opened the message. It was from the librarian. She'd found another newspaper cutting. She'd attached it. Jamie read it with growing alarm.

Having been arrested for the murder of various individuals, the pawnbroker had been sent to prison to await his ultimate fate – hanging. On the morning of his execution, however, he had managed to break free, evade recapture and had completely disappeared from the area.

Lifting his head, Jamie gazed out of the window to find the bright sunshine replaced by dark, foreboding clouds. A storm was coming. In more ways than one.

He sent Sarah the attachment and asked her to meet him. There was now only one place left to go. And Jamie knew, more than anything else, that the pawnbroker would realize this also.

The house.

And now, here they were.

Leaving their bikes outside, they used the same workman's entrance as last time. Treading through the gloom, they made their along the hallway to the large dining room.

The fireplace stood silent and cold, a portal to another realm.

"I must do this," he said, voice sounding tiny and afraid in that huge, empty room. "Tim knew the jewels were the link to everything. If I can discover them, I might bring all of this to an end – and find Tim in the process. I have to. He's my friend."

"I know. He's mine too now." Sarah gave his arm an encouraging squeeze. "I'll be here."

Her confidence and support filled him with courage. Swallowing hard, he dipped his head under the mantelpiece and craned his neck to peer upwards into the blackness. Far above, he could just make out a small sliver of light where the chimney peeped out into the sky.

He'd read how they did it back then, those tiny sweeps, sent up chimneys to clean away the accumulated soot and clinker. How many of them had died? Nobody kept any records back then. Nobody cared. But he knew a lot of them had lost their lives doing this filthy work and now here he was, about to do the same. Gritting his teeth, he wedged his back against one side of the great brick funnel and began to lever himself up, walking one step at a time, whilst maintaining constant pressure against the wall.

It was a long, painful way. Inch by inch he went, the burning increasing in his calf muscles with every step. Every so often he'd stop, not daring to look down, and recover a little of his strength. He winced and groaned as the old chipped and jagged brickwork bit through his shirt into his skin. Another step, then another, determination pushing him on, fatigue ignored. Resolute, he was past caring now about anything except finding the hidden room. The room, which was the key to all of it. Never mind what he'd seen, what he'd discovered in documents, maps and records. If the room, and more importantly the treasure within it, existed, then he'd have the solution to banishing the pawnbroker from his dreams, from his life.

The missing bricks confirmed it.

He'd reached the place where both Bert and Tim had been; the hole, fixed in time, never changing since the moment the bricks were kicked in.

Wriggling himself painfully around the narrow confines of the chimney, he managed to squeeze his upper body through the gap. It was barely large enough to accommodate him. He took a breath, pressed his lips together and, grunting loudly with each movement, using a sort of stop-go method, forced his way into the once secret room.

He rolled and fell onto his hands and knees, sucking in his breath. The skylight afforded a feeble level of illumination, but it was enough for Jamie to make out the dark outline of a large chest. Gaping, he sat still, not daring to believe it was here. So close. So real. Pausing only to wipe his sweating palms on the seat of his pants, he scrambled forward and lifted the heavy lid.

The ancient hinges creaked and groaned as he put his shoulder under the lid and pushed upwards with all his strength. For one terrible moment he didn't think he would make it but, before panic rendered him virtually comatose, he squeezed his eyes shut, straining every muscle to give one last, mighty shove.

The lid fell backwards with a terrific clang.

It was open. Jamie fell back gasping. He'd done it. Success. Victory. He didn't know what to think. But he knew what to do. Inching forward, he looked inside.

The sight that greeted his eyes was beyond his wildest dreams. Jewels and gems of every size and colour glinted back at him. Precious metals, too, and coins that tumbled through his fingers as he picked them up. A whole, wondrous heap of treasure.

Under the array of glitter was something else that caught his eye – a small, plain, unopened manila envelope. He picked it up and for a moment considered putting it back, but curiosity won through. After all, he convinced himself, he'd come this far. His trembling fingers slowly tore open the thin wrapper and he pulled out a single piece of notepaper.

On it, in a most delicate and beautiful hand, was written the following:

My dearest love,
I have set aside here the collected trove of a life's adventuring. From the Indies to Africa, and back to the Orient, my travels have been rewarded with what you see here now. May

*the contents of this chest keep you safe and secure and protect
you from the ills of this wicked world. Remember our words:*

> *'For the years we had together
> and the memories we will always share,
> my heart and soul are yours
> forever.'*

*In truth, this trove is but a poor relation compared to the
feelings that run through me whenever I think of you. Keep
safe, my one, true love.*

At the bottom of the paper a barely legible signature accompanied a date: 1824.

Whistling softly, Jamie sat down on the grimy floor. 1824. If his dreams were real, and there could be no doubting that now, then Bert must have stumbled upon this hoard nearly fifty years or so after it had been hidden away. And that was why the lady was so old. She was the one referred to in the note, the one to whom the dedications on the statue and in the letter had been written.

But why hadn't she used any of this treasure? From what he remembered, she really was very old. Could she have forgotten about it, or did she send Bert up here for the express purpose of bringing it back down for her to sell, or use, or whatever? He didn't know, but inside the chest was a fortune, of that he was certain.

His thoughts were cut off by a single scream from below.

Sarah!

Frantically, he grabbed a handful of jewels, stuffed them into his pocket and slithered through the hole in the wall. In his haste, he grew careless, elbows and knees scraping themselves raw on the sharp and chipped brickwork. He ignored the pain and, as he neared the bottom, he prised free his feet and fell perfectly straight, down into the grate. Without a pause, he bent himself double and moved out from under the mantel and into the room.

Sarah had gone.

Chapter Twenty-Three

… To Those Who Wait

His eyes opened with a snap, his vision filled with an intensely white ceiling. He blinked a few times. The sight remained unchanged. As he struggled to sit up, pain lanced through his head and he fell back, desperately trying to remember. Where was he? How had he got here?

Tim had no answer.

The room was small, cold and airless. Again, this time much more slowly, he tried to sit up, preparing himself for the pain. But it was nothing more than a dull throb now and he looked around. There was no window and only a tiny bedside lamp to chase away the blackness. Opposite was a door. He contemplated opening it, but what would he do if it were locked?

He lay on a simple camp bed. Pressing his fingers into his eyes, he tried to remember. Something. Anything. Gradually, disjointed images came back to him, like fragments from an old, long-forgotten film. The old hospital. Something had compelled him to go there. An unseen force, like a magnet, drawing him in. Stepping into the dark corridor, confused, disorientated, he'd taken a few steps and then…

Then there was a blackness deeper and more penetrating than the building's interior.

He'd been hit on the head. And brought here, to this room. But why?

He swung his legs over the edge of the camp bed and prepared to sit up.

The door flew open, almost ripped from its hinges.

Silhouetted in the door frame stood a man, his huge cloak swirling as if caught by an invisible breeze, his broad-brimmed hat pulled down hard, concealing his features. But Tim knew who it was. The man from his nightmares.

The pawnbroker!

* * *

Jamie found Sarah outside, sitting on the top step, looking out at the once beautiful ornamental gardens. Relief leaving him speechless, he slumped down beside her. She appeared as if in a dream, eyes strangely vacant, not focusing, blank, staring.

He waited. There was no need to rush, not now. Now, everything was going to be all right. Reaching into his pocket, he pulled out a pendant. A simple gold heart. It was huge. He hefted it in his palm. This piece alone must be worth at least –

"Jamie." Her voice sounded detached, distant, as if she herself were not the owner of her words. "Jamie…"

Hastily returning the gem to his pocket, he turned to her, eyes locked on her mouth. It quivered. She was close to losing control. "What is it, Sarah? Why are you… ?"

Slowly she turned and considered him in silence. Her eyes welled up, a tear tumbled down her cheek and her lips trembled even more. "Oh, Jamie…"

A sudden, frightening changed occurred. In an instant, without any warning, she sprang at him, gripping his lapels, shaking him violently. "Oh Christ, Jamie – I saw him!"

He tried to force her hands from his shirt, but it was impossible; her strength was unnatural, overwhelming. "Sarah! Sarah, for God's sake, who did you see?"

She reared backwards, her mouth wide open, holding onto him as if her life depended on it. "He was looking in through the window, staring right at me. Smiling. That smile. It scared the hell out of me. I screamed and ran. I wanted to get away and I didn't care about you or anyone else. I just had to get away. But when I got outside, he'd gone. Vanished. I checked the side of the house, but there was no sign of him. No sign. No sign... Oh God!"

She released him and, as if all the strength had left her body, she fell backwards and wept, face in hands, body rocking like a small child. Lost. Devoured by fear.

Jamie, his throat as tight as if someone was squeezing the life out of him, could do nothing but stare.

He was here. The pawnbroker. He'd followed them. Somehow, some way, he'd crossed the bridge between past and present. In those few days since Jamie and Tim had stumbled across this place, a new, terrible phenomenon had been created. One beyond reason or understanding. And he was the one responsible. No one else.

And no one else could end it.

"He wants these," he muttered and pulled out a fistful of jewels. Slowly, her tears subsiding, Sarah dragged away her hands and stared at his hands, at the glittering jewels and pieces of gold hanging between his fingers. Neither spoke.

There was no way of telling how long they sat there in silence. Time itself seemed suspended, as if it, too, was waiting for something monumental to happen.

And then, it did.

Tim's piercing scream cut through that frozen moment like an ice-pick, shattering everything, returning them to the present with all its horrors.

With his hair wild, sticking out at every angle as if charged with electricity, Tim burst out of the main door and stood panting in front of them. Scrambling to his feet, Jamie took a step towards his old friend but stopped as Tim raised a warning hand.

They looked into each other's eyes.

"I'm sorry, Jamie," said Tim, his voice low, laced with fear. The tough, cheeky, carefree Tim had gone, replaced by a tired and terrorised little boy. He sobbed, body shuddering, and shook his head, dragging his eyes from those of his friend. "Try and forgive me but… I had no choice. No choice."

"Had no choice about what?"

"Bringing you here."

"What? When? What are you talking about, Tim?" He went to take another step, but Tim shot out his hand again, his tears suddenly ceasing, his eyes hard now. Vicious.

Jamie stopped, waited, held his breath.

"He knew, you see. He's always known. Even before you did."

Jamie frowned and looked down at Sarah, who said nothing, simply stared as if in a daze.

"You're a receiver, Jamie," Tim continued. "Like me." He teetered forward, legs wobbly, as if he, too, were in some sort of trance. "Didn't you ever stop to think and ask yourself why we became friends? Of all the people in the school, why would I choose you to be my closest," he swallowed, looking down to the ground for a moment, "bestest friend?"

Jamie felt his own eyes filling up. He shook his head, not daring to accept Tim's words. "You're saying you were forced to become my friend?"

Tim nodded, raising his face to meet Jamie's eyes.

"Who by?"

"You know."

A heavy stillness settled around them. Above them, the iron sky grew darker, the thick clouds threatening to break open and send the rain pouring down. Wasn't the past always like this?

Grey figures in grey streets? Was this what was happening now, past ages overwhelming the present, making it all one?

"You had the dreams, too," Jamie said at last, "but…" He took a breath. Did he really want to know the truth? "You mean you had them long before we came here?"

"For years. So many, I can't remember when they started. I didn't understand them at first. It was only when I was older, when I came to your school and met you for the first time, that it all began to make sense. It was then that he came to me, told me to become your friend… that you were stronger than me, more reliable."

"Because I could connect with Bert."

Tim nodded, his face heavy with sadness. "Yes. And I couldn't. It was all you, Jamie. All you."

"But… but I didn't know about this," he gestured towards the house. "I'd never had a single dream, a single thought about this place until…"

"Until, for some reason which neither of us understood, we cycled up here and found it. "

"We were guided here."

Tim shrugged. "By memories… ghosts… desires… call them whatever you want. It doesn't matter now. He's controlled everything from the start. And now he's won." Tim's face crumpled, his anguish complete, and he fell heavily to his knees, body shaking with great, heaving, uncontrollable sobs.

Utterly lost, with no idea what to do, Jamie looked from one friend to the other. They were both gripped in anguish and when he looked again at Tim, he found his friend staring blankly ahead with the most pitiful look in his eyes.

But that was nothing compared to the face of the apparition standing behind him, its bristling, lumbering form cloaked in a long, ragged coat, features cast in deep shadow by the wide brim of its hat. When it spoke, its voice rumbled as if from a deep well, and was filled with such malevolence it chilled Jamie to the very core of his soul.

"I want what is mine."

The words acted as a release for Tim, who reeled towards the others.

All three huddled together. No more tears. They all waited for what they knew was to come.

Taking the first of several heavy steps forward, the pawnbroker snaked out a long, thin arm towards them. But it was no ordinary arm. Grey-fleshed, veins of the deepest, virulent purple protruding like ropes, the limb appeared corrupted with age. And then it spoke again, words rattling in its throat. "Give me what is *MINE!*"

They recoiled, the two boys yelping in horror. But it was Sarah who found the resolve and the courage to answer this thing standing before them – for *thing* it was. No longer human, it stank of decay, of the earth which gave it succour. It was not of this world.

Sarah stood up and held its gaze. "But it isn't yours!" she spat defiantly.

For a moment, the pawnbroker wavered, head cocked, not understanding her words. He appeared perplexed, confused that she should have the impertinence to even contemplate speaking to him. Then came a cackle of disgust. "Pretty girl. Clever girl. Brave girl." He took another step, his threat clear. "Don't be a stupid girl, not now. Give me... what is ... *MINE!*"

He leaped forward, arms reaching out to seize her.

But now Jamie reacted. Galvanised into action, he grabbed Sarah by the arm, yanked her out of the pawnbroker's reach and screamed, "*Run!*"

And they did, all three of them, bounding down the worn steps and racing through the ancient, neglected gardens, never looking back, skirting around the large ornamental fountain, heading towards the trees that framed the sprawling estate.

Beyond was another, much smaller fountain. As they drew nearer, the impossible became reality.

Jamie ground to a halt, stumbled and fell, taking Tim with him. Sarah let out a terrified scream and Tim, caught by surprise, senses in disarray, rolled forward and came to a stop... at the feet of the pawnbroker.

Climbing to his feet, Jamie gazed in disbelief at what he saw. How could it be? They had run like demons but, like the demon he was, the pawnbroker had somehow managed to overtake them and now he stood, his cackling voice ringing in their ears, his hands firmly locked around Tim's throat.

"I'll make you an offer," he hissed. "I was often in the habit of offering much less than what things were worth. How else could I make a living? Well, today is different. I think today I will offer you more than those jewels are worth. Today, I will offer you the life of this boy against what you have in your pockets."

Around them, the night developed, thick with dampness. Deep and brooding, the trees swayed in the light breeze, but no other sound broke the oppressive stillness. It was as if the world and everything in it was waiting. Waiting for Jamie's answer.

And of course he had seen it all before.

His dream, the worst dream. In the garden of Mr Taylor's house and what had happened to Josh. Josh, murdered by the pawnbroker. And now, here it was being replayed, only with different characters in a different setting. Another time.

"No," he muttered. "No, this can't be happening." He wanted to blank it out, to wish it all away, to wake from what this had to be – another nightmare. So real, but a nightmare nevertheless. What had he read about waking yourself from nightmares? That you had to pinch yourself, to snap yourself back to reality?

He tried. Ridiculous though it seemed, he dug his fingers into the soft flesh of his arm and squeezed. He bit down on his lip and yelped, but when his eyes opened, nothing had changed. Tim was still struggling in the pawnbroker's iron grip and those black, sunken eyes of the fiend burned with a red fire, just as they had always done. This was too terrible to accept but, surely to God, history didn't repeat itself like this?

In the dream, they were saved by a scream, the scream of Mrs Taylor whose fateful intervention saved Bert and Annabel... but not Josh. Only where was Mrs Taylor now?

And then, a gradual realisation flowed over him. It was like a soothing balm, it felt so good. In the dream, Josh had been murdered in the grounds of Mr Taylor's house – but this *wasn't* Taylor's house! This was the old woman's house! History was not being repeated.

And yet, the scream came nevertheless.

But it wasn't Mrs Taylor's voice ringing out across the night. It was Tim's. The pawnbroker lifted him as easily as a rag doll and hurled him over the rim of the ornamental fountain, plunging his head into the filthy, stagnant water. Kicking and floundering, Tim fought desperately, but it was useless. The pawnbroker was too strong, his cold-steel fingers pressing down, keeping him under the frothing water. Tim battled, arms waving, beating the water, but still the pawnbroker held him.

"Trust me," he hissed, glaring at Jamie over his shoulder, "I will end his wretched life."

Sarah and Jamie acted as one, charging the pawnbroker as if possessed, both clawing at his arms, kicking furiously at his shins. Jamie's fists pummelled the powerful man's ribs. Nothing worked. The fiend's hold on Tim never slackened and his response to their assault was a chilling peal of laughter, ringing out through the night, mocking them, taunting them.

Breathless, Jamie stepped back. "Leave it, Sarah!"

She snapped her head around, bewildered, wide eyes full of questions.

"Step away," he ordered. She did so, recognising something in his voice. A strength. From his pocket, he pulled out the bunch of jewels. "It's these you want," he yelled and swung away, holding the sparkling gems aloft, even the darkness unable to extinguish their lustre. Rushing to the larger fountain, he flung the jewels towards the black, still water. They arced through the night air like a thin, tiny tracer and landed with a single plop into the murky depths.

With a roar, the pawnbroker released Tim and blindly raced towards where the jewels had fallen. Jamie stepped back and saw Sarah helping Tim, coughing and spluttering, to his feet.

The sound of the pawnbroker plunging into the water in his hopeless search for the gems caused them all to look up. Jamie, a new sense of courage coursing through him, moved closer. Through the gloom, he made out the fiend's frantic efforts to find the jewels. Floundering through the depths, arms scooping back the water, he searched while a constant droning growl emanated from the pit of his stomach – a sound of despair and anger, horrible, preternatural, not of this world. Not of this time.

Watching as if mesmerised, all three gazed upon the despairing sight. When the pawnbroker quite unexpectedly slipped and disappeared under the surface, Jamie almost wanted to rush forward and help. But he held himself in check. This thing, whatever it was, wanted them dead. So, he stood and watched, saw the pawnbroker rising up, gasping, his mouth open in a soundless scream, before being dragged down once more. Down into the depths of water that was deep… dangerously deep, impossibly deep. For one awful moment, the pawnbroker seemed to regain his footing, only to slide back down in a great splash. The more he struggled, the more he lost control. Soon, he screamed, "Help me! For pity's sake – I cannot swim!" But the water engulfed him, his words muffled in the frothing, surging cauldron.

They looked on, unable to move. It was as if they were transfixed, restrained by a mysterious force that prevented them from helping even if they wanted to. But they didn't. They watched in an almost nonchalant manner, without reacting, as the pawnbroker thrashed away frantically, his voice shouting out as before, seemingly forever.

And then, as suddenly as it had begun, all was still. In the dim, murky darkness, the only discernible feature was a shape lying face down and lifeless in the inky blackness of the water.

None of them knew how long they stood there. Jamie first became aware of someone approaching when a torch beam came dancing through the blackness, picking out their faces. A voice followed. A voice he knew. His mum, shouting, "Jamie – Jamie, are you all right?"

Suddenly, it was as if the whole world had arrived. Lights flashed, radios crackled, men and women in uniform milled around, voices barking at one another. And Jamie's mum was holding him close, kissing his head, reaching out, beckoning Sarah and Tim to join them. All of them huddled together, crying with relief, the ecstasy of being alive.

"Mum," spluttered Jamie at last, as if emerging from a deep, hypnotic state, "he's here. *He's here!*"

Pushing past her, he rushed to the fountain to find him. The pawnbroker. He had to know, he had to be certain. He peered over the edge.

The water lay still and flat, reflecting his face back at him as he strained to look beneath the depths. Aware of a figure close beside him, he snapped, "A torch! Please, give me your torch!"

The policeman passed it over without question. Sarah and Tim were with him now and as Jamie turned the beam towards the water, all three stared into silvery surface.

Nothing.

No sign.

As if a thousand years had failed to leave their imprint, the water remained still and tranquil. No sign of the pawnbroker remained. Only the memory of his desperate fight for life.

Jamie's mum hovered behind them, her voice soft and gentle, reassuring. "What is it? What are you looking for?"

"Look!" cried Sarah, pointing. The nearest policeman followed her finger and, without a pause, stepped into the icy cold depths, right up to his waist. Reaching down, he muttered something, and then brought out his hand and held it aloft like the winner of a sporting contest.

In his fist was a bunch of glittering gems.

No one spoke. Dumbstruck, they merely watched as the policeman climbed out, the water dripping from him. He was grinning.

He was the only one.

Re-focus

Across the centuries, men and women surrendered their most precious possessions in order to gain something they believed would change their lives for the better. All had been consumed by desire, the lust for wealth. And the creature had given them a chance to taste a tiny morsel of this most choice of fruits.

Failure had almost always followed.

Blinded by the folly of their weakness, they could not see that life held so much more than mere riches. But as the centuries turned, and material possessions became the singular most important thing in life, the creature thrived. Even now, with its most recent disciple destroyed, it licked its lips, relishing the opportunity to feed upon other lost souls.

Perhaps it would take more time, or require a wider sweep, but eventually others would come to him, their avarice limitless, their greed total. And it would begin again. The harvesting of souls

But not here and not now. These persons were beyond its powers now. Fleetingly, there had been the tiniest flicker of hope, but this had been dashed. They could all get on with their pathetic, normal lives. All that remained now was to seek out other lost souls, elsewhere.

It was euphoric at the thought.

Chapter Twenty-Four

Words in the Night

After coming down from his bath, Jamie sat with his mum on the couch, staring at the empty television screen. Dad had been and gone, relieved that everything was back to 'normal'. Jamie had laughed at that, but not out of amusement. How could things ever be 'normal' again?

Mum made him hot chocolate and he sipped at it in silence as she busied herself somewhere, cleaning something. Sarah was coming to visit again tomorrow. And Tim. All thoughts of them being banned from seeing each other were forgotten now. Normal service had been resumed.

Jamie sniggered and sighed deeply.

How could things ever be as they were, he asked himself again? The whole adventure had left such an effect on them. Jamie felt changed; older, wiser. More sensible. No, he thought sharply, never that. Never sensible again. Sensible hadn't brought him anything but despair.

He put his head back and stared at the ceiling. If he thought about it, now that it was over and he was safe in his own home, with Mum so close and Sarah and Tim his friends once more, it had been good fun. The dreams, the finding out, the history, the pawnbroker… He shuddered at the thought of *him*. No, that bit definitely was not fun, but everything else had been… exciting?

Is that what he could call it? What about the deaths, though? What about Mr Morris? The police still hadn't closed the case. The murderer, they said, was still out there.

Could it actually be true?

The telephone rang and he sprang up and ran into the hall to answer it. It was Tim.

"Hi," began Jamie, trying to sound enthusiastic. Tim didn't. His voice sounded distant, vague and unsure. Perhaps he was suffering from the trauma of what had happened, thought Jamie. "Are you all right? You sound..."

"I'm fine. I'm just, you know..."

"Yeah, I understand. Are you still coming for tea tomorrow? Sarah is."

"Yes. I'll be there."

"Good. I'll ask Mum to get some Hobnobs in. You like them, don't you?"

"Jamie."

Jamie stopped. There was something in his friend's tone. Something he recognised. Like the voice he used when he emerged from the house... and then Jamie just listened to what his friend had to say. When he'd finished, Jamie replaced the receiver and stood staring into space.

He felt his mum behind him and he turned. Her face had that 'Mum wants to know what all that was' look on it. So, he took a breath. "That was Tim. His mum went to the library. Did what we did, me and Sarah. She found something. Something we didn't."

Mum's expression never changed. She took his hand in hers. "I was with her."

Jamie looked at her, open-mouthed. She nodded at his surprise.

"I was going to tell you," she continued, gently, "but not until tomorrow, after you'd had a good night's sleep." She gave a long sigh. "But, as you've already found out..."

"No," Jamie said quickly, "Tim didn't tell me the details, just said his mum had discovered some stuff that was really scary. He didn't say any more. Neither had she."

"Perhaps I shouldn't then?"

He looked at her imploringly. "Please, Mum. It's the only way to put a stop to all of this."

She nodded, making up her mind. "All right." She took one of his hands and held it gently in her own, her mouth set in a long, thin line. "It was an impulse thing. What you and Sarah had done seemed the obvious way to find some answers. Both you and Tim were haunted by those dreams, so… Anyway, we got to talking, Tim's mum and I, and we decided to go to the library together. We don't really know each other very well, but…"

She caught Jamie's impatient look and carried on. "Well, we went, that's the important thing. We found some old newspaper records from the same time as your census stuff. It took us ages, but eventually we got it – a report of the whole nasty affair. It seems that after the pawnbroker had eluded arrest, apparently for the second time –"

"Yes, he'd escaped the hangman's noose. The librarian told me."

"Yes, well, it seems that this pawnbroker went back to the big old house, to find out where the jewels where hidden, once and for all. He confronted the old lady, who stood up to him, bless her heart. Anyway, he was followed. By two children…"

"Called Bert and Annabel?"

Mum nodded and Jamie felt a buzz in his heart. "He took them by surprise, forced Bert to go up the chimney, to the secret room, and bring down the jewels. He only brought back a handful. Then there was a scuffle and in the mayhem, the jewels were thrown into the fountain and…"

"Don't tell me!" Jamie's hand flew to his mouth. "The pawnbroker drowned trying to recover them?"

Her blank look was enough. Jamie clamped his hands to the side of his head. "I don't believe it," he gasped. "You mean the whole thing we went through was repeated, but it was us this time?" He shook his head. "I don't believe it..."

"Jamie," his mum's voice was soft and reassuring, "the police found no evidence of a body in that fountain."

"So what are you saying, Mum? That we imagined it, all three of us?" He shook his head. "That's impossible."

Mum shrugged. "No, I don't think you imagined it. Perhaps you were a witness to an event so violent, it left its imprint on the atmosphere. You said as much yourself, Jamie, many times."

"Ghosts? No, Mum, we touched him. He had Tim under the water..."

"There were no marks around Tim's throat. I know, I spoke to his mum." She looked down. "She also told me Tim has been having dreams for years. They'd been to doctors, psychiatrists, the lot. Then a spiritualist. You know what that is, don't you?"

"Of course. They get in touch with the dead."

"Those who have 'crossed over', Jamie." She looked annoyed for a moment, but it passed as quickly as it had come. "I... well, it's a long story, but... well, I've had similar dreams."

"*What*? When? You never told me, you never said anything about –"

"I know, I know," she said, cutting him off. "I should have said. But it was all so long ago and nothing like this. Dreams of lost relations, friends. That sort of thing. But you... you made a *link*, Jamie – a connection!"

Jamie shook his head sadly. It was all too much to take in. Then the light went on in his head. "But not all of it was a dream, was it? The houses were real. And the jewels, they are real."

"Yes. The police got them down from that little room. The whole lot." She played with the hem of her skirt. "I can't begin to explain it all, Jamie, I don't think anybody ever can." She smiled. "But at least some good will come of it."

She smiled again, this time at the frown creasing his face. "According to the police, the jewels will be sold off and the proceeds put towards a good cause. If Tim's mum and I have anything to do with it, it will go towards cancer research, or a scanner at the Royal. You see, we also found out something else. Mr Taylor? He died, in 1917. Of cancer."

She walked with him up the stairs to his bedroom. At the door, Jamie stopped and looked. "But what about Bert and Annabel?"

Mum shrugged. "We couldn't find out anything about them. No mention, except that little entry in the census. Mr Taylor was mentioned by name in the newspapers only because he was such an important businessman. Perhaps there's a biography, or even an autobiography we could find, that will answer some, or all, of our questions."

She helped him into bed, tucking him in as only mums can, making him feel like a little boy again. She leaned over him and kissed him lightly on the forehead. He didn't pull away. "But all of that we can save for another time. For now, tomorrow and the next day – and for the rest of this holiday, young man – I want you to concentrate on having a good time. And try to forget all about this business."

She stood up and went over to the main light switch. "Sarah and Tim will be over for tea tomorrow." She gave him a wink. "That Sarah's really nice, don't you think?"

Jamie mumbled something incomprehensible and turned over as Mum switched off the light.

Alone in the dark, Jamie's eyes closed, not to dream this time, but to pray that this night, the nightmares would stay well away from his door.

But then, just as exhaustion overtook him, his door suddenly creaked open again and Jamie peered out to see Mum standing by his bed.

"I forgot to say," she began, stroking his head, "you know Dad came round? He was so worried about you. Well, we got to talking and... would you mind terribly if *he* came over for tea as well?"

Jamie sat bolt upright, crying out with joy, and threw his arms around his mum's neck, squeezing her as hard as he could. Now he knew for certain that the nightmares would stay well away. For good.

The End

About the Author

Stuart G Yates is the author of a eclectic mix of books, ranging from historical fiction through to contemporary thrillers. Hailing from Merseyside, he now lives in southern Spain, where he teaches history, but dreams of living on a narrowboat in Shropshire.